Doris Free

BY CARA BROOKINS

ILLUSTRATED BY
ANN BARROW

For my grandmother, Doris: Your endless generosity, dedication, and compassion continue to be my inspiration. Thank you for your vivid memories and wisdom. You brought Doris Free to life. — C.B.

For Scott — A.B.

Mondo Publishing would like to dedicate this book to Ann Barrow, a kind person and talented illustrator, who passed away shortly before completion of the book.

Text copyright © 2006 by Cara Brookins
Illustrations copyright © 2006 by Ann Barrow under exclusive license
to Mondo Publishing

For information contact:
MONDO Publishing
980 Avenue of the Americas
New York, NY 10018
Visit our website at www.mondopub.com

Printed in China

09 10 11 12   PB   9 8 7 6 5 4 3 2

1-59336-333-8 (PB)

Designed by Jean Cohn

Library of Congress Cataloging-in-Publication Data
Brookins, Cara.
  Doris Free / by Cara Brookins ; illustrated by Ann Barrow.
    p. cm.
  Summary: On a farm in 1931 Wisconsin, ten-year-old Doris befriends her struggling neighbors and tries to find ways to help them survive--both in body and spirit--during the Depression.
  ISBN 1-59336-333-8 (pbk.)
  1. Depressions--1929--Wisconsin--Juvenile fiction. [1. Depressions--1929--Fiction. 2. Hope--Fiction. 3. Neighborliness--Fiction. 4. Farm life--Wisconsin--Fiction. 5. Wisconsin--History--20th century--Fiction.]   I. Barrow, Ann, ill. II. Title.
  PZ7.B789788Dor 2006
  [Fic]--dc22   2005013471

Contents

CHAPTER 1

Saturday Morning

Doris stretched sleepily in the dim morning light. She pushed herself to the edge of the feather tick and slid her thin, pale legs out from the warmth of the patchwork quilt. She was careful not to wake her sleeping sister Arla, who was wrapped snugly on the other side of the old wooden-framed bed that their pa had built from pine boards. Arla snored softly with only a mop of curls visible over the faded blue edge of the quilt.

The cold Wisconsin air stung Doris's bare legs and goose pimples popped up on her skin. Her toes curled as she stepped onto the cold floorboards. She dressed quietly, putting on her faded yellow play dress and pulling long white stockings over her knobby knees. Raking her fingers through her bobbed brown hair, Doris considered running a brush through but decided against it. Her straight, ordinary hair would look the same whether she brushed it or not. She tucked her hair behind her ears and clamped her hard-soled leather shoes under one arm to silence her early morning getaway.

Doris often awoke in the dim hours of the morning and sat by the fire in the stillness, especially in the winter, when her family was trapped in the house together for months on end. It was her private time, before her sisters Victoria, Jena, and Arla woke up. Tiptoeing softly down the long staircase, she carefully hopped past stair number seven with its noisy creak.

In the living room, she nestled into a quilt on the threadbare orange sofa by the old black woodstove. The family had lovingly named the potbellied stove Bertha after old aunt Bertha who had a round middle and squat legs like the stove. This March morning Bertha had grown cool, so Doris unlatched the door with a thick mitten and laid a small log in the glowing coals that remained. She knew Bertha would spark up soon with this dry fuel.

Fluffing her hair around her ears, Doris settled in, alone with her thoughts. She curled her legs under her and pulled the patchwork quilt up around her ears. Although she was strong from the work that she did on the farm, she was still a thin girl. Her blue eyes were thoughtful, and she always looked on the verge of a smile. Her ears, which stuck out through her short hair, had made Doris self-conscious when her hair was still long and she wore it pulled back in a ponytail. Since she'd had it cut, Doris had developed the bad habit of tucking the shorter strands behind her ears. She was desperately trying to break this habit for fear that it would cause her ears to protrude further.

Doris had a button nose that sprouted a scattering of light freckles in the late summer. But now, after a long winter, there wasn't a single dot on it. Doris had studied the noses of her schoolmates and was certain hers had the best shape. But she was also sure that her ears stuck out more than most children's. In reality her ears were quite unnoticeable, but she had convinced herself otherwise.

Doris peered out the window. In the dim morning light, she could just make out her father's brown wool hat hanging on the spike by the barn door. He was out milking the cows, as he did every morning. *Today is Saturday,* thought Doris, *which means that Pa will dump the cream into the churn for us girls to pump into butter.*

Doris didn't mind making butter, but she would much rather use the cream to top off a big bowl of berries—her favorite treat in late summer. It would be months before the berries were ripe; the bushes hadn't even sprouted leaves yet. Doris longed for the warm days to come, especially for school vacation to begin in mid-May. Doris was ten years old and in the fifth grade. Her marks in school were always decent, but she was terribly shy and preferred her family's secluded farm to the noisy school playground.

Doris's thoughts danced lazily, jumping from one topic to the next as she sat by Bertha's now warm glow. Some mornings she thought about important things, but usually she just let her mind wander. She dreamed of faraway places and exotic people. Sometimes she made up stories of ordinary people doing amazing things. Other times she simply sat and thought about her own life and the many people who touched it.

Doris realized that her time spent alone in thought was coming to an end when she heard Arla bouncing noisily out of bed and running to the closet for her dress and stockings. Doris looked to the stairs and, as expected, Arla's messy mop of curly brown hair poked out of their bedroom door. Then Arla was thundering down the stairs, stepping noisily on creaky number seven, which was certain to awaken the rest of the family.

Arla, at seven, was very different from Doris. They shared the same long, thin frame, blue eyes, and mousy brown hair, but Arla did everything quickly and noisily. Her nose was larger and rounder, but Doris envied Arla's ears, which were delicate and didn't stick out at all. Arla never tucked her hair behind them, and Doris was certain that was the secret. Doris smiled as Arla hopped the rest of the way to the sofa on her one shoed foot. She had tied knots in the other shoe's laces and was working frantically to loosen them so she could make her morning run to the outhouse.

"Get your coat on, Arla, and I'll work the knots out of your laces," Doris said with a giggle.

"Thanks, Doris," Arla yelled over her shoulder. She tossed the shoe on the sofa and ran to the closet for her old, gray wool coat.

"Got it," Doris announced, handing the shoe to Arla, who shoved in her foot and ran out the back door. Arla tripped twice on the untied laces in her haste to get to the outhouse. Doris smiled at her sister's disorganized rushing about. Sometimes she wished that she could charge through life the way her younger sister did. Nothing worried Arla, and she hurtled from one moment to the next with an enthusiasm that was downright contagious. Doris, on the other hand, thought things through carefully and planned out everything.

Upstairs, Victoria and Jena were dressing quietly. Doris could hear their low voices through the thin floorboards. She couldn't make out all of the details, but it was obvious they were continuing the argument that had begun when the cold weather arrived: Who would get to wear the brown play dress and who would have to wear the blue one? The girls' winter play dresses were almost threadbare and all had been heavily patched, so it was doubtful that one of them was any warmer than the other. Yet week after week, the argument about who would get to wear the warmest dress continued.

The two oldest sisters were very much alike. Not only did they both have wavy blond hair and blue eyes, but they also had matching tall, slim figures. They were both beginning to round out a little, and Jena was only an inch taller than Victoria. The resemblance didn't stop there; it went clean through to nearly every thought and mannerism. They both twirled their hair around their left index finger when they were nervous. When they spoke, it was hard to tell who owned which voice if they weren't within sight. Ma had always said that they were "twins born a year apart."

Before long Jena appeared at the top of the stairs wearing the brown cotton dress that they had decided was warmer. Her hair was pulled back in a braid and tied off with a piece of white fabric that showed off her perfect ears. Down the stairs she came, avoiding the creak with a light leap. She went into the kitchen to light the stove for breakfast. Victoria, wearing the blue dress, a frown, and an identical braid, stepped extra hard on stair number seven and walked straight to the kitchen.

At thirteen and twelve, Jena and Victoria were expected to do a great deal of the cooking and other household chores. They had all grown up in the kitchen at

Ma's skirts, so they were comfortable with these tasks. They especially enjoyed cooking in the winter months when the stove warmed the house and made them all feel cozy.

Ma was the last one up, which happened only on Saturdays. It was the one day of the week that she let the chores wait until the sun came up. She smiled at the girls, her blue-green eyes still sleepy, and asked, "Is Arla out already?"

Just then the back door opened and in flew Arla, who tossed her coat and kicked off her shoes. Ma smiled at Arla's reckless way of entering the house and, like Doris often did, she tucked behind her ear a strand of long brown hair that had come loose from her bun. She then exclaimed in mock sternness, "Get those things into the closet, young lady. We have a breakfast to make."

Turning toward the other girls, she said, "Doris and Jena, you had better gather the eggs and tend to the chickens. Make sure that they have some water that isn't frozen solid. Victoria, you head down to the basement and bring up the bacon and the bread. Arla, you start pumping some water for Pa's coffee and to wash the eggs with."

Each of the girls set off to do their respective chores with a "'Kay, Ma."

CHAPTER 2

Chores

Doris was relieved that Ma had sent her to tend to the
chickens. She hated the basement. It was one of the scari-
est places in the house, second only to the attic door at the
top of the stairs. Besides, she liked the chickens. As soon as
she opened the door to the coop, the big gray-black rooster that she called King tottered down the ramp and eyed
her expectantly. He was the oldest rooster and had lost
some of his toes to frostbite years before, so he wobbled
along on his disfigured pink feet like a baby learning to
walk. Doris scolded, "Hold on, King, I didn't bring all of
this food just for you. Wait for the hens."

Soon, more than twenty chickens of different colors
and shapes had exited the coop. They pecked and clucked
around Doris's feet as she scattered cracked corn and
oyster shells. They ate quickly and scratched at the ground,
hoping for an early beetle or worm. Then they hurried
back into the coop and sat on their nests. Doris always
tried to gather some of the eggs before the chickens
finished feeding and returned to their nests.

Jena, who had stood back while Doris scattered the

feed, now picked up the large water basin and dumped the ice out of it saying, "I'll go to the pump for water while you gather the eggs, Doris." Then she skipped off quickly, her braid swinging back and forth under the rim of her knitted hat. Jena was almost as scared of gathering eggs as Doris was of the basement. One of the hens had pecked her hard on the hand the previous winter and she had been scared of them ever since. It hadn't helped that her older cousin Herman had told her how lucky she was because chickens usually went for the eyes. Anyway, there was always so much work to be done on the farm that it was never hard for Jena to find other jobs to do while one of her sisters gathered the eggs.

Thankfully, Doris didn't know the reason behind her sister's fear of the clucking hens. She picked up the egg basket, strode confidently into the coop, and began gathering eggs. Doris always talked to the hens as she reached under their soft, warm bodies to remove the treasure they guarded. Most days the speckled hens were her favorites, with their spattering of white and black feathers, but today the fat brown hen caught her eye. She never named any of the hens, because she had learned as a young child that they often disappeared before a big meal. They were farm animals, not pets—except for King, of course, who had become a sort of family mascot.

Even though they weren't pets, Doris still enjoyed being around the animals. She admired the fat brown hen's smooth, shiny feathers and gave her a gentle pat. The hen tilted her head and watched Doris suspiciously, letting out a shower of noisy clucks when she was robbed of her egg.

Pa had marked several eggs in each nest with a paint mark. These were the eggs that were to be left to grow and develop into chicks—the first spring hatchlings. Doris gathered sixteen eggs and was certain that the fat brown hen had given her a double-yolker. She wrapped the red and white cloth from the egg basket over the eggs, carefully keeping the possible double-yolker to one side for her own breakfast.

By this time, Jena had finished filling the water basin and was secretly relieved when Doris sauntered out of the henhouse with both eyes still in her head. Jena saw that a few of the monster chickens were still pecking the ground looking for bits of corn, but she looked away quickly. Jena and Doris walked back to the house, chatting happily about how the mounds of snow by the barn seemed to be melting quickly and how spring would soon come, bringing its warm weather and beautiful flowers.

As they entered the kitchen, the warm air was welcome to their ice-cold toes and shivering knees. Arla was standing on a stool in front of the kitchen sink, playing in the basin of warm water she would use to wash the freshly gathered eggs. Ma had the coffeepot ready and was just pouring the steaming coffee. It was 1931, and coffee was an expensive luxury that Pa rarely expected. In December he had received some as a gift from his brother, who lived in Minnesota, and they had used it sparingly to make it last. The last few weak cups would be drunk this weekend. Doris would miss the coffee's strong, sweet smell when it was gone.

"Let's see how many eggs you gathered today,"

Ma said, taking the basket from her daughter.

"I've got sixteen," Doris announced proudly, "and a sure double-yolker from the fat brown. Can I have it, Ma?"

"Sixteen? That's wonderful, Doris! Spring is definitely on its way. Yes, you can have the egg from the brown . . . seems fair. Go and put them all in the basin for Arla to wash." Then Ma turned to Victoria. "Is that pan ready for the bacon yet?"

"Yes, Ma, I'm putting it in now. Should I fry it all?" Victoria asked.

"Might as well. There will be no more for a while," Ma said matter-of-factly. She and her family were used to going without things, as these were hard times with the Depression on. They were all good at making do with what they had and knew many others who were far less fortunate. They had a house to live in, plus animals and a big garden that provided them with food for the table. And with spring just around the corner there was a lot to plan for—it was no time to sulk about what was gone.

"Jena, as soon as Victoria pours off some of the grease, you start the eggs in the big skillet," Ma directed. But the routine was well established, and the girls all knew what was expected of them. Jena was standing by the sink waiting for Arla to finish the eggs when Pa came in from the barn. They knew that something was wrong when they saw that he had forgotten his hat in the barn and was wearing his work gloves in the house—two things that almost never happened. His brow was creased in a worried frown, and he didn't greet the girls with the usual cheerful banter that he reserved for his "ladies of the household." Instead, he hurriedly grabbed some old blankets from the top of the storage closet and headed back out to the barn without a word.

All four sisters looked worriedly at Ma, who went straight to the closet for her coat and boots. "You girls call out when breakfast is ready. I'm going to see if your pa needs any help in the barn," she said over her shoulder on the way out the door. Her brow, too, was knit with worry.

CHAPTER 3

A Confession

"I bet one of the cows is having a calf," Arla said in a hopeful whisper, her eyes wide with anticipation.

"No, none of them are ready yet, Arla. It's way too early. Something's wrong," answered Victoria, shaking her head, her blond braid swinging from side to side.

The girls finished preparing breakfast with hardly another word. They couldn't afford to lose any of the animals. Each of them hoped that Ma and Pa would come back soon and fill them in on what was happening. Soon the table was set and the last egg fried, but still no word from the barn. The older girls looked at each other, not sure if they wanted to know the answers to the questions racing through their heads.

"Ma said to call when we were ready," announced Arla. She was oblivious to the unspoken worries of her sisters.

"I'll call her," Jena said. As the oldest, she felt it was her duty to take charge when no one else wanted to. Jena moved swiftly to the back door and called Ma and Pa in for breakfast, hoping they would put an end to the morning's mystery.

Ma came in first, and the angry look on her face surprised the girls. They looked at one another, each girl trying to remember what mischief she had gotten into that could have caused injury to one of the animals. One after the other, they shrugged their shoulders as nothing came to mind.

Ma sat down at the table and said, "Your pa will be along in a minute. Buttercup has a terrible infection and fever. It seems that someone decided to let that stray dog loose after Pa's instructions not to untie her. I expect whoever is responsible to explain herself after breakfast."

Buttercup was everyone's favorite cow. She was a fat brown milk cow with a velvety black nose and the biggest brown eyes anyone had ever seen. All of the girls were worried about her, not just because the family needed the milk, but also because she was like a pet to them.

Doris began to squirm in her seat, and not only because she was worried about Buttercup. She was worried about herself as well, because she was the one who had let the scrawny dog off of her leash. It wasn't like Doris to disobey her father, but the pup had looked so sad. She had only meant to let her loose for a little while, but then Arla had come along and suggested they play dolls and . . . Oh, how could she have forgotten? And now poor Buttercup was suffering because she had gone off to play instead of watching the little dog.

"Maybe the dog chewed through the old rope we tied her with," Victoria suggested hopefully, interrupting Doris's thoughts.

"I don't see how that little dog could hurt a big ole cow like Buttercup anyhow," Arla interjected through a mouthful of bacon and eggs.

"It would seem," Ma explained, "that the little dog likes to chew things and also to chase things that wiggle. As you might recall, Buttercup has a tail that wiggles quite a lot, and that pup has chewed her tail right to the bone. An infection is already setting in, and it is important that we get her healthy fast. Spring will be here soon, and the insects and warm weather will make it harder for her to fight off the infection."

"What can we do?" Jena asked with a hopeful voice.

"Well, your pa cleaned and stitched the wound. I took him some clean rags to bandage it with, but I imagine he'll need some clean strips of cloth and ointment this afternoon to give her another treatment. It looks like she will lose part of the tail. That will make it hard for her to swat away the stinging deer flies this summer. Let's just hope that her fever stays low and she is able to fight off the infection. We certainly can't afford to lose any animals right now."

Doris knew all too well how important the animals were to them. The winter had been long and hard, and they had used up almost all of their supplies. No one even dared talk about how life would be next year if things didn't improve. The Depression meant hard times for everyone. In a way that made it easier to bear—it didn't seem so bad to be poor and go without nice things when everyone else was in the same boat.

Sometimes, to Doris, it all seemed like a game. They tried to come up with new and interesting ways to make the things they could no longer afford buy. And when they did get something special, like the thick bacon on her plate, oh, how much more they enjoyed it! Little things

meant a lot to them now. And most of all, they had learned that the only things that really mattered were the people in their lives. Family was more important than all of the things that they had to do without. That was one of the reasons why Doris felt so bad about Buttercup. She didn't want her pa to be disappointed in her. She wanted everyone to be proud of her, but she knew they'd be angry with her for disobeying orders not to untie the dog.

Suddenly, the double-yolker didn't taste too good anymore. Even the slab of bacon on her plate had lost its appeal. Guilt is a rotten thing, and it gets worse the longer a person keeps it inside.

Ma noticed that Doris was looking down at her plate and pushing around her egg, her fork rarely making it to her mouth. She guessed that Doris had something to do with the dog being let loose and that she was feeling terrible right about now. Ma knew her children well, and she knew it would be best to let Doris admit her mistake on her own and take responsibility for the problems that her carelessness had caused. She sighed deeply; her own breakfast had lost its appeal while she watched the struggle going on inside Doris.

Jena broke the silence, skillfully changing the subject. "Ma, can we go look for rags by the dump today? The snow is melting and there should be some newly uncovered stuff that no one has gone through yet."

With a tight smile, Ma nodded yes. She hated to have her children digging in dumps. *How terrible that we've come to this*, she thought, *but we can't afford to buy new fabric, and goodness knows that the rags will come in handy.*

The girls took pieces from the best rags—old shirts

and dresses, mostly—and sewed them into quilts. But they rarely found anything in good enough shape for quilts anymore. The Depression was hitting everyone hard, and rarely was anything thrown away that had any use left to it at all. They had only managed to piece together one quilt this winter.

They used the oldest rags to make rugs. The girls cut the clothes into long strips and sewed them together end-to-end. Then they would roll the strips into giant colorful balls. Ma would then weave the strips into circular rugs. The different strips of cloth made colorful swirls on the rugs, which were thick and lasted well.

While Ma did this, Doris enjoyed her own weaving—she'd weave stories about the people who might have worn the clothes that were becoming their rugs. Ma and the girls loved Doris's tales of the wealthy, exotic, and famous people who might have owned the rags before them. Because of these stories, they'd come to call the rugs "story rugs."

They needed new rugs now. The kitchen rugs were worn so thin that they no longer kept the girls' toes warm against the cold floor. They'd already made seven rugs that winter but had to sell them all in order to buy supplies like flour and salt. Ma knew that if the girls could find some decent rags today, they could get some rugs made before winter ended. Because once spring arrived, every waking moment would be filled with the seemingly endless chores created by the new growing.

Arla was so thrilled about the visit to the dump that she didn't notice that Doris was quieter than usual. Jena and Victoria noticed however, and looked at each other with raised eyebrows. They'd figured out that Doris must be to blame for Buttercup's injury. They felt badly for their sister. Ma and Pa rarely punished the girls and probably wouldn't punish Doris for this either, but it was clear that Doris was already punishing herself.

"I'll bet Buttercup will be all better by supper time," Jena said reassuringly to no one in particular. "Remember when old man Zeke's bull broke through our fence and stuck Buttercup with his horns? She was only still for one day before she was back out taking care of her calf. She is tough, and she knows that we need her. She'll be better in no time."

Doris looked up and smiled weakly. When her eyes met Jena's, she could tell that her sister knew she had let the dog loose. Her cheeks burned red hot with the guilt. Jena tilted her head toward Ma, signaling to Doris that she should tell Ma the truth and make things better. Doris sighed; she knew Jena was right. She wondered why it was always so hard to admit that you had done something wrong. She never had any trouble telling Ma when she did something good. It seemed to her that both things should be equally easy to tell, because so many lessons were learned in both cases. In fact, she usually learned more from doing something wrong than doing something right. Still, it sure was hard to get the words out.

Arla was jabbering away about the things she wanted to plant in her row of the summer garden when Doris suddenly took a deep breath and, in what sounded like one long word, interrupted with, "I-did-it-Ma-I-let-the-stray-dog-loose-from-the-rope-I-only-meant-to-untie-her-for-a-few-minutes-while-we-played-but-I-forgot-

about-her-and-never-tied-her-back-up-I'm-sorry."
Doris's eyes were filled with remorse for what she had done, and each of her sisters felt awful for her. They all looked at Ma expectantly, holding their breath and awaiting a response. Even Arla was silent.

Ma frowned at Doris. She knew that her child had already learned her lesson and that there was no reason to lecture her, yet it was her duty to reinforce the lesson as best she could. "Doris, you know that your father and I like that little dog too, but when you are told not to do something it's with good reason. We don't make up the rules just to make life difficult for you. That pup is a stray. If we are to keep it, then it needs to be taught the rules of the farm before being allowed to run around. Your pa and I will have to talk about this and see what is to be done. For starters, as soon as you finish your breakfast go and relieve your pa so that he can eat something himself. You will not be going with your sisters to the dump today."

Doris nodded her head without looking up from her plate. She continued to shuffle her egg around on the well-worn glass surface. She didn't even mind staying home today. Maybe if she helped Pa they could save Buttercup. Maybe she could make everything better after all. She certainly felt better now that she had admitted her mistake and would be helping to fix it. She nervously pushed her hair behind her ears again.

"You'll have to eat now, Doris, so you can go help your pa," Ma said with a gentle nod towards Doris's plate. "You can carry his plate out to him when you're finished." Then she changed the subject in an attempt to relieve the tension that had silenced the girls. "So, Jena, what makes you think the dump will have some good rags today?"

Victoria answered for her sister, who had a mouth full of milk. "We've been cooped up in the house all winter, Ma, and so have most of the folks around here. Stuff has been piling up at the dump for months with no one able to get to it, what with all the snow we've had. Much of it will still be covered, but who knows, we could get lucky!"

"I see, so you really just want to get out of the house for a while, do you? Well, at least this will give you something useful to do. Take the wheelbarrow with you and remember to watch out for broken glass—it can cut clean through your shoes." That was true, especially considering that their shoes were worn so thin that they were little more than fabric.

Doris chewed the last of her bacon and started wishing that she could go with her sisters. It certainly would be nice to get out and away from the farm for a while. While summertime meant lots of adventures and exploring, in the winter all the girls did was go to school and do chores. And sometimes the snow was so deep that they couldn't even leave the house for days at a time. Next time, Doris told herself. And the next time there would be even less snow so they'd be that much more likely to find something useful.

Standing up and gathering her dishes, Doris interrupted her sisters' excited chattering. "I'll go out and see if I can help Pa now." She set her dishes in the sink and then put on her wool coat. "If you find a button at the dump, be sure to bring it. I sure would like to have a real button instead of tying strips of cloth to hold my coat closed."

Doris walked into the barn carrying a plate of eggs in

one hand and a speckled-blue tin coffee cup in the other. Her father crouched next to the sleepy old cow.

"How's she doing, Pa?" Doris asked in a whisper.

Pa patted Buttercup's round middle then looked at Doris, who was standing near the doorway looking upset and guilty. "I take it you are the one who let the stray loose? Well, I'm sure your mother has already talked to you about it, but you know that the rules around here are to keep everyone safe, even the animals. Now I think the worst Buttercup is going to suffer will be from the flies she won't be able to swat away this summer due to her shortened tail. She is going to be fine, Doris. It is a good thing that we got the medicine on her right away."

Pa stood and gathered up the extra rags. He walked over to Doris and, laying a hand on her shoulder, told her to clean up the horse stalls before she came back to the house. Doris nodded and went to the back of the barn for the pitchfork. She began scooping the soiled hay from the stalls, while Pa sat on a bale next to Buttercup and ate his breakfast.

CHAPTER 4

Treasures
Found

"**L**ook at this one, Victoria!" Arla shouted, waving the worn flannel shirt she had found at the edge of the dump. The girls had been right; much of the snow had melted, and items that had been hauled in before the snow came were now revealed. They had discovered an old crate overflowing with clothes, and they couldn't believe that anyone would throw away such useful things. Most people in town had so little that they reused whatever they did have. It was unusual to find so much useful fabric in the whole dump, let alone in one spot.

"Wow, Arla, that's perfect for a rug, and it has buttons on it, too! Wait 'til Ma sees all of this—we'll be busy sewing right into planting season. I think we've found enough for a whole quilt *and* some rugs. This is just like a birthday, isn't it?" The girls were giddy with excitement. They had never found so much at the dump. "One of us had better haul this wheelbarrow home now and then bring it back. I think we'll be able to fill it up twice today." When no one volunteered, Jena offered to do it.

Arla looked up from the pile of coffee cans she was digging through, an eager grin lighting her face and her hair a mass of wild curls. "See if Ma will let you bring some food back with you for lunch, Jena."

Victoria and Jena looked at each other and rolled their eyes over Arla's huge appetite. She thought about food nonstop and could eat more than any of her sisters, even though she was the youngest—and the skinniest.

"I'll ask, but Ma will probably want us home for lunch," Jena answered. She began the mile-long walk back to their house. The trip would take longer than usual because the wheelbarrow was so full and heavy. To make matters worse, the dirt road was scattered with holes caused by the melting snow. Jena pushed the wheelbarrow in a zigzag pattern the whole way back to avoid the holes. Her arms were aching by the time she reached the house.

Ma was hanging the wash out on the line when Jena came up the driveway. "My goodness, girl, look at all that you've found today! We could have used this sewing to keep us busy through the winter, couldn't we have?" Ma held up an old pair of pants and smiled at the large button that was the perfect size for Doris's coat. "Where are your sisters?"

"There's still more, Ma. I came back with this load while Arla and Victoria pile up whatever else they can. Oh, and Arla wants to know if I can bring some food back with me for lunch."

Ma smiled, her eyes sparkling from the good news. She felt lighter and freer than she had in months. "Of course she does. Arla always wants whatever food she can talk me out of. I'll get some bread and cheese and some of the left-over roast from the basement, and you girls can have sandwiches. Get a quart jar from the cabinet and pump some fresh water into it so you all have something to drink."

Ma turned, and as she went into the house, she wiped a silent tear of relief from her cheek. She had worried for so long about how she would manage to keep her family clothed this summer and how they would buy enough seed to plant the fields. They had eaten some of their seed store to survive the winter. Now with all that the girls had found, they could make rugs and maybe even a quilt to sell. Good fortune had come their way.

CHAPTER 5

A Stranger

Doris finished cleaning the horses' stalls and gave them fresh hay and oats to eat. It was hard work, and it took a lot longer to do by herself than it did when her sisters were helping. It was also less fun because there was no one to talk to except the horses, and they weren't very good at keeping up their end of the conversation.

Doris loved the horses dearly. The Frees owned four, which was a lot for one family. The horses helped with the farmwork and pulled the sleigh in the wintertime. But they didn't have to work as hard now that Pa had a tractor. He was lucky because many farmers in Tomah still did all of their work with big plow horses. After Pa got the tractor, Doris was relieved that he sold only the two big plow horses and kept the others for riding. In the summer the girls loved riding the horses around the farm, and sometimes Pa would let them ride over to a neighbor's house to play.

Doris got out the stiff-bristled brushes and started brushing down the horses. She began with Rain-in-the-Face, her favorite. His warm belly felt good on her cold hands. He was such a dark brown color that he looked black in the dim light of the barn. His face was spattered with white spots that looked like drops of white rain. This, of course, was how he'd gotten his name. Doris brushed his coat until it was shiny and smooth and then nuzzled his velvety snout and whispered of the adventures they would share in the coming summer.

Just as Doris finished brushing the last horse, she heard a noise outside the back door of the barn. At first she thought it was another stray dog, but then watched as the black metal latch slowly turned and the door opened. Blinding sunlight flooded in, and all Doris could see was a small figure slip in and disappear into the front of the barn where the feed grain was kept. Doris could hear her heart beating loudly in her ears. She crouched down in the stall and peered through the slats. She pushed her hair behind her ears and listened for movement. Nothing. Had she imagined it? No, she was certain she'd seen someone—a small someone—enter the barn. *Arla!* thought Doris. *I'll bet they've returned from the dump and Arla has snuck in to try to scare me. Well, I'll show her. I know where she is, but she has no idea where I am!*

Doris slipped off her shoes and soundlessly made her way to the front of the barn. As she neared the grain storage area, she heard some rustling. She could hardly suppress a giggle as she imagined the look on Arla's face after getting the fright of her life. Doris jumped out from behind a low wall and yelled, "GOTCHA!"

But it was Doris who got a fright when, instead of her sister, a dirty boy jumped and screamed in surprise. The two children stared at each other in wide-eyed silence for a moment while both caught their breath. The thin boy

wore a pair of old, patched brown trousers and a tan work shirt that was much too big for him. His toes poked out from the pieces of flat leather that were tied to his feet for makeshift shoes. He didn't have socks or a coat, even though it was a nippy March day in Wisconsin. His dark hair was matted and dusty, and it needed to be cut.

Doris could see that his thin frame was shaking with fear—or maybe he was just cold. His large brown eyes never left hers as she looked him over and tried to figure out what he was doing in the barn. She noticed that his small button nose was similar to her own, and she wondered if he, too, got freckles across it every summer. His skin was so pale that it was almost transparent. His eyes, framed with the longest and thickest lashes Doris had ever seen, were beginning to shift nervously back and forth.

Despite his fear, the boy found his tongue before Doris could think of anything to say. "I'm sorry, miss. I didn't mean to take anything that you might need. My aunt and I are awful hungry, and I didn't know where to get some food. I haven't anything to trade. But I could do some work for you, maybe. Please don't tell your folks that I've taken anything. My aunt would whip me something awful if she found out."

Everything he said had been true except the part about his aunt whipping him, but he hoped it would bring him some sympathy. His pale lips trembled as he tried to read the expression on Doris's face and wondered if she would scream or run or tell on him. He began plotting his getaway just in case. They were about the same size, and he could probably push past her to the door if it came to that. He couldn't afford to get into any trouble.

Doris's brain felt foggy. She was having trouble putting all this together. She hadn't even realized that the boy was stealing from them until he had mentioned it. She wondered where he had come from. *The railroad isn't far,* she thought. *Maybe he came in on a railway car.* He'd never been to school or even gone shopping in town, that was for sure. Tomah was a small town and anytime someone new came, the news traveled fast. It was obvious he was poor and probably hungry, too. He seemed honest enough, though, and it was clear that he was ashamed of stealing. Taking a deep breath to calm her fears, Doris asked quietly, "Who are you? Where do you live?"

The boy was still uncertain about how this girl might react, so he answered cautiously. "I'm Danny. I live just down the road with my aunt. I've been stayin' there since my parents died last year. We aren't thieves, but the winter has been so long, and there hasn't been any food left for a while now. I've had to make do with what I can find for us. Auntie doesn't want any trouble, so I don't tell her how I get stuff. She doesn't even ask me anymore."

Doris watched the boy suspiciously. He looked like he was telling the truth, but she wasn't sure about trusting someone who'd intended to steal from her family. Then she noticed that he was cradling something bulky in his left arm. "What have you got there?" she asked, pointing to his bundle.

Opening a soiled rag, the boy showed her two fresh eggs. They were large and Doris wasn't sure if she had missed them that morning or if they had come from somewhere else. "I've got some eggs. They're from the geese out by the pond. I haven't taken any eggs from you, honest. I was taking some grain, hoping that my aunt could make some bread with it or some warm mush. I set some traps for rabbits, but I've only caught one. I really don't know much about trapping. My aunt is too old to do much herself. Well, she's not that old really, just tired a lot. She tells me how to do things. I'm going to plant us a garden soon. Then I'll be able to take care of both of us," he said, puffing his chest out with pride in a way that made Doris feel sorry for him.

"Why haven't I seen you at school or heard about you in town? What's your aunt's name anyhow?" Doris asked, her suspicion growing over the boy's unlikely story.

"I don't go to school," Danny said defiantly. "And my Aunt Winnie doesn't get out around other folks much. She says she doesn't trust 'em. I tried to talk her into going to town for the winter play—my folks used to take me to them back home and I remembered that there was always hot cocoa to drink—but Winnie wouldn't go. Did you go?"

Doris nodded her head that she had, but she was getting even more confused. She knew she was supposed to be angry with this boy for stealing, but she was starting to like him. He liked to talk, that was for sure. And anyone who liked to talk that much would have trouble holding their tongue long enough to hide a lie. Knowing that his aunt was Old Lady Winnie explained why she hadn't seen nor heard of him since his arrival. No one ever heard from Old Lady Winnie. She had been hiding in her rickety shack on her dried-up farm two miles down the road ever since her husband died five years earlier.

Doris knew that a lot of folks in town had treated Old

Lady Winnie badly after her husband passed. He had been a gambling man and owed money to almost everyone. He was big and mean, and no one dared collect anything from him while he was alive. But once he died, they went to his farm and took what they thought he owed them from his poor widow. Winnie'd never had many friends in the first place because of her mean husband, but after the towns-folk had taken everything, except for the shack, she stopped going out altogether. Now folks left her alone— many of them because they were ashamed of taking from her. The local children made her out to be a witch and told terrifying, made-up stories about her.

Danny shifted nervously from foot to foot. This girl was too quiet for him. "So are you gonna tell on me Miss . . . ? Hey, what's your name anyhow?"

Doris hadn't decided if she was going to tell on him or not, but she knew from her experience earlier that morn-ing that keeping things from her parents wasn't something she liked doing. Somehow, though, this seemed different to her.

"My name is Doris. I don't want to tell on you, Danny, but I don't like lying to my parents either." She tilted her head and considered the boy carefully. He was looking down at his dirty toes. Shame masked his face. Then she remembered the hot eggs and thick bacon she'd eaten that morning and felt guilty about having so much when he, obviously, had nothing.

"Okay," she sighed, "I won't tell. But you have to promise not to steal from us ever again. I'll try to help you come up with a better way to get food. Is that a deal?" Even before she'd finished asking the question, the answer was clear from the beaming smile that lit up his pasty face. They most definitely had a deal.

Now, Doris would have to figure out just what she was going to do about Danny and his hungry aunt . . . .

Suddenly they heard distant voices coming from outside. Danny looked at Doris in a panic. "Don't worry. You stay here and I'll go see who it is, okay?" Doris reassured him as she headed toward the barn door. She was still in her stocking feet, and pieces of hay collected on her stockings as she walked. She opened the door just enough to peek out and saw her sister and her mother talking excitedly over a wheelbarrow full of rags.

Danny watched with wide, frightened eyes as Doris walked past him and back to the horse stalls. "What are you doing?" he whispered.

"I'm going to get my shoes, so I can go out and find out what my ma and sister are doing. You wait over there behind that low wall," Doris said, motioning toward a corner of the barn with one hand and pulling on her shoes with the other. "I'll be right back."

By the time Doris reached the front of the house, Ma and Jena had already gone inside. Eyeing the wheelbarrow of rags with interest, Doris walked up the steps and opened the door. She paused, looked back toward the barn, and went in.

Jena was sitting at the table resting and nibbling on a crust of bread. She was tired from the long walk and from pushing such a heavy load, but she smiled excitedly when she saw Doris. "Did you see how much stuff we found, Doris? We have enough to make a whole pile of rugs, and Ma said we could probably start a quilt because some of the clothes are in good shape!" Then some of her excitement died away. "I wish you could have come with us Doris. It . . ."

At that moment Ma opened the door that led up from the basement and Jena fell silent. "Let's pack up lunches for you to take back to the girls, Jena . . . and Doris, you can eat here. Then you and I can sort through this clothing and get it washed out."

The girls quickly packed up the lunches, and Doris made a larger-than-normal sandwich for herself, discreetly wrapping it and setting it aside. When Jena left again for the dump, Doris turned to Ma. "I'm going to eat my lunch out in the barn with Rain-in-the-Face. Then I'll come back and help you with the rags, okay?"

Ma nodded her head and went back to her cleaning. Doris ran out of the house, letting the front door slam shut behind her. With barely a pause, she grabbed a thick wool shirt from the top of the pile in the wheelbarrow and hurried back to the barn with the large lunch clutched in her hands.

CHAPTER 6

Picnic at
the Dump

As Jena neared the dump, she could hear her sisters' cheerful chattering. She left the wheelbarrow on the road-side and carried the picnic lunch over to where her sisters were still searching through the thawing mounds of junk. "What did you find while I was gone?"

Arla looked up from the piles of broken bricks and rubble that she and Victoria sat on. "Did you bring something to eat? I'm starved."

"We found some more clothes and piled them up over there near the road. We even found some red handker-chiefs that Ma can use to make summer halters for us! I don't think we'll find anything more today, but we sure did good, didn't we? I'll bet Ma was surprised!" Victoria said proudly and excitedly.

Jena looked in the direction Victoria had pointed and saw a large pile of clothes. Victoria's face was framed with straggles of blond hair that had escaped the once neat braid. She looked dirty and tired, but there was a smile on her face. They would have a hard time getting this load back to the house in just one more trip, but that was a wonderful challenge to face.

"Ma was very pleased. We won't be able to finish sewing all of this into rugs and quilts before planting season. We will be busy long into next winter. This is the best spring ever!" Jena truly thought they must be the luckiest people in town. She was so happy that she tingled with joy.

"Is there something to eat in that bag, Jena?" Arla asked impatiently, holding a small, brown glass horse with a broken tail that she had found.

"Yes, silly! Ma made us a picnic lunch." Jena knew Arla was too young and carefree to realize how much this find would mean to their family during these hard times. Even she and Victoria didn't know as much as they thought they did about the difficulties their family would have faced without this to pull them through, but they knew enough to be proud and happy with their find.

The girls ate and laughed and played until they were full and exhausted. They looked around a little more, but didn't see much else of interest. Arla found a small metal cabinet that they all agreed to take back to Doris. She liked to save things, and the paper box in which she was currently keeping her collections was falling apart. They felt badly that she had to work today while they had an exciting day away from the farm, and they all knew that forgetting to tie the pup back up was a mistake any of them could have made.

Victoria squinted at the sun as it lazily made its way toward the horizon. It was still getting dark early. Spring had not yet arrived in Wisconsin. "We'd better start heading back now. Ma will want our help with supper."

"Good, 'cause I'm starved," stated Arla matter-of-factly.

Jena laughed at Arla's insatiable appetite. She looked at Victoria and said, "You are going to have to push the wheelbarrow this time. My arms are still sore from pushing it all the way home and back earlier."

The wheelbarrow was made of thick metal and it was heavy even when empty. The front wheel was also metal, and it had dime-sized bumps on it to give it a little traction on the sandy roads. But the going was still hard. The girls had seen a wheelbarrow at the Dime Store in town with rubber on the wheel. They had been fascinated with it and imagined how much easier it would be to haul things in.

As it turned out, the load didn't fit in the wheelbarrow, so Jena and Arla each had to carry a bundle while Victoria pushed the wheelbarrow with the rest in it. They wrapped the spillover in two large shirts and then slung the bundles over their shoulders like happy little elves.

They were all in good spirits as they walked home. The only thing that could have made them even happier was if Doris had been with them.

CHAPTER 7

Picnic in
the Barn

Blinking, Doris tried to focus her eyes in the dim light of the barn. The bright sunlight had left her seeing spots. She saw a shadowy figure walking toward her and was startled when she realized it was much too large to be Danny, whom she had left hiding behind the wall. It was Pa!

"Doris, you did a good job with the horses. The stalls look clean and their coats are gleaming from the brushing you gave them." He paused to evaluate the strange expression on Doris's face, then continued when he decided she was just flushed from her run to the barn. "I just went out to the shed to have a look at that stray dog again. She isn't rabid, but she sure is a playful thing. I'm afraid that we'll have to find her a new home. She's much too interested in the tails of other animals to stay here. I just don't have the time to train her, but hopefully someone else will."

Looking down at her shoes, Doris tried to calm her racing heart. Pa hadn't even noticed that she had a bulge in her coat where she had tucked the thick shirt. She tried to look sad about the stray dog, but really she had much more important things to think about right now. She wondered if Danny was still crouched behind the low wall by the feed. He must have been terrified when her father came into the barn. She squinted in concentration, trying to see if there was any movement coming from that part of the barn.

Interpreting her squinted eyes as sadness, Pa tried to comfort Doris. "I know you girls really like that frisky brown pup, but we have to make sure all the animals are cared for, and that pup is just going to cause problems. Would you like to be the one to find her a new home?"

Doris nodded her head in agreement. Eager to have her father leave the barn and move on to his other chores, she changed the subject. "Ma said I could eat my lunch out here by the horses. She has some more bread and meat for sandwiches inside if you're hungry."

Pa realized that she didn't want to talk about the dog, so he removed his work gloves to go in for lunch. "That sounds really good right now." He hung his tough, leather work gloves on the rusty nail next to the barn door, placed his hat on his head, then turned back to Doris. "Isn't it still a little cool out here for a picnic?"

It was indeed cool in the shady barn when she wasn't working up a sweat. Doris shrugged. "Nah, it feels like spring is in the air, and since we've all been stuck inside for so long, it feels good." With that, she turned and headed toward the horse stalls. She had to make a big effort not to look behind the wall for Danny as she passed by—she didn't want Pa to suspect anything.

Doris heard the barn door shut and realized that she had been holding her breath. She exhaled a huge sigh of relief, waited a moment to be sure that Pa was gone, then bolted to the other side of the barn to see if Danny was still there.

Doris poked her head around the wall. Danny looked up from his hiding place, his eyes still wide with fear. "I thought for sure that your pa was gonna find me. I stayed right here and tried to think of what I should do or say to save my life if he found me. And I . . ."

"It's all right now, Danny. He's gone to the house for lunch. Then he usually falls asleep for a little while, so you're safe. I brought you this." Setting the bundle of food and a jar of water on the top of the wall, Doris pulled the shirt out from under her coat. "It's wool and will keep you warmer than what you are wearing. I got us some lunch, too. Let's eat, and then you had better get out of here before Pa comes back."

Doris and Danny divided up the sandwich and started eating. Two of the barn cats kept trying to steal pieces of meat from the children's sandwich, and their playful antics had Doris and Danny laughing until tears streamed down their cheeks.

The children enjoyed talking and laughing together. They had quickly become friends. They talked about the sick cow, Buttercup, and the stray dog that had hurt her. Danny mentioned that he had always wanted a dog and that maybe his aunt would let him take the pup if he could find a way to feed it. Maybe it would be a good hunting dog. Doris didn't mention that a hunting dog wasn't much good without a gun to hunt with. Instead, she told him she would help him keep the dog.

Doris also told Danny about the dump and all of the stuff that her sisters had found there. He was excited about the possibility of finding useful things and said he'd go as soon as he could. Doris secretly hoped that her sisters hadn't found all the clothes at the dump so that there would be something left for Danny.

After they'd finished eating, Danny said he had to go home. His aunt would be hungry, and he had the goose eggs for her. Doris filled the wool shirt with some oats. They weren't much good for Danny and his aunt to eat, but they could feed their scrawny milk cow, Jo.

The children promised to meet the next afternoon. Then Doris went out to make sure that her father was nowhere in sight before telling Danny that the coast was clear and it was safe for him to leave.

CHAPTER 8

An Early Night

When Victoria, Jena, and Arla arrived home, it was already getting dark. By then Doris and her mother had sorted and washed the rags from the first batch. The clothes hadn't had enough time to dry completely on the outside clothesline, so Ma brought them inside and hung them on the winter line that stretched over Bertha. They would be dry enough after supper to remove the buttons and start cutting.

The girls were exhausted and hungry. They had taken turns pushing the wheelbarrow and carrying the bundles all the way home. The rutted dirt road made the trip even more difficult. Ma and Doris piled their junkyard treasures in the corner of the porch so the girls could wash up for supper.

Doris had peeled some carrots and potatoes for a stew. To add flavor they used the last of the roast that had gone into their lunchtime sandwiches. They were lucky to have had such a good potato crop last year; they still had a large pile in the basement. Sometimes the girls got tired of eating them, but they knew the spuds were healthy and filling, so they were grateful to have them. They weren't as lucky with the carrots. They were almost gone, and the few that remained were getting rubbery. The girls were as anxious as their parents for spring to arrive so that they could plant more vegetables.

Ma urged the girls to finish the supper preparations. "The soup is almost ready, girls. You get the table set while I slice some bread. Doris, did you finish churning that butter?"

"Yes, Ma. I scooped it into the big green bowl and put it in the pantry. I'll go and get it." The butter had been hard for her to finish without her sisters around to give her a break from the pumping of the churn. Doris also had worked hard in the barn, so now her arms were sore.

Pa came in from the evening milking, and they ate supper together. They were in good spirits and talked and laughed easily. Pa told them that Buttercup was still sick from the infection, but that he thought she would recover completely. They talked about the animals and about the warm weather around the corner. The girls chatted about summer vacation and how they would enjoy the break from school, but also how they would miss their school friends. Many of them lived miles away, so they usually didn't get to see each other during the summer.

It was Doris's and Arla's turn to wash the dishes. Ma poured the water that had been warming on the stove into the dishpan. Doris soaped and rinsed the dishes, and Arla dried them and put them away, chattering all the while. But Doris's mind wandered, and she didn't hear much her sister said. She was thinking about Danny and wondering if he and his aunt had anything warm to eat that night.

Had they eaten the goose eggs or saved them for break-fast? She wondered if they talked and laughed together at mealtimes. She also wondered what had happened to Danny's parents. Doris realized she was lucky to have her family all together.

"Well, did you see them or not, Doris?" Arla asked for the second time.

"See what, Arla?" Doris felt guilty that she hadn't heard her sister the first time.

"The buttons, silly. We found three brass buttons that will be perfect on your coat. I guess Ma must have washed that shirt. Are we done with the dishes?" Arla looked around the kitchen and back at the table. "Good, let's see if we can start on the rags now. I'll get the scissors."

Doris suspected that the shirt Arla was referring to was the one she had given to Danny. She hoped that her flighty sister would soon forget all about the shirt.

Jena and Victoria sat with Ma on the sofa, carefully cutting the buttons off the rags. Pa sat in his chair, puffing on his pipe and reading the *Farmer's Almanac*. Sometimes he would tell them stories, and sometimes the girls would make up their own fanciful tales. Doris was the best story-teller of them all, especially when they were working with rags. Arla couldn't wait to hear her sister's tales about the people who once wore these clothes.

Tonight, though, they all seemed to be lost in their own thoughts and remained quiet, while they worked. Even Arla was quiet, and that was certainly unusual. It was-n't long before, one by one, the girls started to yawn. But Doris was still wide awake. She couldn't stop thinking about Danny and how lonely and sad he must be having lost his parents and then moving to a strange town where no one even knew that he existed. There must be some way she could help him.

They probably don't even have enough wood to warm their little house or to cook with, thought Doris. Danny wasn't big enough to chop wood, and the townspeople had taken the tools from the farm anyhow. It was probably a cold night for them tonight. Maybe Danny would be a little warmer now with the wool shirt that Doris had given him.

The girls all went to sleep early that night. Living on a farm meant lots of hard work, and this day had brought a great deal of excitement along with the work. It had been a good day for everyone. Well, except for Buttercup.

CHAPTER 9

A Blossom
of Hope

As Danny walked home that evening, he thought about his new friend, Doris. He had been so frightened when she caught him stealing, but she had turned out to be kind. She had promised to help him come up with ways he and his aunt could survive besides by taking things from others. He hated stealing and knew that his parents would not have approved. His life had changed so much since they'd died. Now that he had finally found a friend here, he realized just how lonely he had been.

Danny had gone to the dump after saying goodbye to Doris. When he'd arrived the other Free girls were still there, so he'd waited until they had left before digging in himself. He'd found a few things that would make life a bit easier for him and his aunt. There was an old copper cooking pot—it had a few big dents in it, but the bottom was still flat enough to sit on the cook stove. He'd also found a few articles of clothing. Most of them were too worn out to wear, but he was hoping Doris would show him how to make the rag rugs she'd told him about. He'd seen many other things that he thought might be useful, but it had become late and he'd needed to get home to help his aunt, so he hadn't been able to look them over properly. He would go back to the dump soon.

"Gracious, where have you been, boy? I've been looking out this window half the day wondering what you had gotten yourself into." She noted the bundle he carried. "What have you got there? Have you been a good boy?" She didn't want the boy to take things and get into trouble, but she didn't ask many questions because they were so hungry and had so little.

Danny decided not to tell Winnie everything about his day. She was so wary of others and angry at the townsfolk that he didn't want her forbidding him to see his new friend. He tested the waters, not realizing that, as much as he liked to talk, it was almost impossible for him to keep anything secret. "I went down the road a bit and ended up meeting a girl named Doris. She was real nice and told me where there's a dump, and I found all this stuff there." He lifted the cooking pot so she could see the rags that he'd stuffed inside of it.

Danny grinned and puffed his chest out with pride when Winnie smiled lovingly at him. She had never told him how much better her life was with him around. She had been alone for so long that she found his constant chatter a welcome change from the years of silence. Winnie didn't have any children of her own, nor did she have many friends. She felt alive again for the first time in many years. Unlike Danny, Winnie didn't talk much, so the boy was mostly unaware of the positive effect he had on her.

"That is a good pot, boy. I wish it was full of stew, don't you? And those rags will make some good rugs indeed. Do you know how to make rag rugs?" She looked down at his dirt-caked feet and continued without waiting for an answer. "Mercy, but you are a mess, child. Get some wood from the porch and we will warm some water on the cook stove to clean you up."

Danny's grin quickly turned to a scowl, "Aw, gee, do I have to, Winnie? I'm really not that dirty at all." He glanced at his feet. The skin was cracked and calloused from the cold air—it had been so long since he'd had a pair of shoes. His toes were indeed quite dirty, but he knew that a bath would leave him cold and wet and that it would take hours to warm up again in the drafty house. There wasn't much wood left in the pile to make a fire. In an attempt to change the subject, he presented Winnie with the food he had found that day. "I got you some eggs, Winnie. And look, I got some oats, too. Oh, and this wool shirt will keep me lots warmer than that old rag I've been wearing." He held up the shirt, and the three shiny brass buttons glinted in the candlelight.

Winnie carefully took the precious eggs and set them on the countertop with the oats. "That is wonderful, child. I will see what I can make us for supper while you get your bath started." She smiled at the look of disappointment that came over his face when he realized that changing the subject hadn't worked.

Danny walked toward the porch to get some wood for the fire. "That's okay, Winnie, I already ate today. Doris shared a big sandwich with me." He turned to Winnie with wide, dreamy eyes, "And it had real beef in it and bread made with yeast! I never tasted anything so good in my life. Doris's family has a real farm."

After Danny's bath, Winnie used the warm bath water to clean the rags that he had found. She wished they were good enough to make into a quilt, but they were worn too thin for that. Maybe she could sell a rug, though, and buy some seeds for the garden that Danny wanted to plant so badly.

They sat together, Danny shivering in the cold with his wet hair. Winnie had made a soup of sorts out of some left-over meat from a goose they had managed to catch. She had put the eggs in the thin soup to thicken it and give it some flavor. She wished they had enough flour and eggs to make noodles, but she had been making fried flat bread out of the little flour that was left. They had run out of yeast mid-winter. They had gotten used to the bland flat bread, though, and it was pretty good with the soup. Winnie made sure that Danny ate well, despite his declaration that he had already eaten that day.

They were both happy that night—full of dreams for the future—and they slept snugly. Winnie had put an extra log on the fire. With spring just around the corner, she figured they could use up the last of the firewood without fear of freezing to death.

Morning dawned bright and clear and full of hope. Winnie and Danny sat by the fire, and she showed him how to carefully remove any buttons still on the rag clothes. Danny sorted the buttons into groups by color and put them in glass jars with other buttons Winnie had saved. He loved all of the different colors and shapes of the shiny buttons, and he imagined that the jars were filled with sparkling jewels. Next time he went to the dump, he would look for some buttons to add to this collection.

Winnie began cutting the fabric into long strips that were about an inch wide. She cut in spirals up the sleeves of the shirts to create long pieces of fabric. Danny quickly caught on and took over the cutting while Winnie sewed the strips together to make one long piece. Then she wound it into a large colorful ball that could be sewn or woven into a rug. It took them most of the morning to finish the rags. Winnie was pleased with the result.

"We should get two nice rugs out of this large rag ball, Danny. We have done well." She smiled and realized that for the first time in many years, she was dreaming of a better life—a life that wasn't marked by hunger, cold, and loneliness. Yes indeed, she felt better than she had in years. Winnie wondered about the little girl who had befriended Danny. She had given him food and told him about the dump where he could find useful things. There were still good-hearted people in the world after all. How good it was to know that. She didn't know many people anymore and wondered whose child this Doris was.

Danny smiled with pride as he sat and rolled on the large rag ball. He pushed the straggles of dark hair out of his eyes. "You will finally have a warm rug under your feet, Aunt Winnie. Is it all right if I go out now? Maybe I can find some more eggs."

"Yes, you may go out—but not far as it is getting dark." Then she hesitated for a moment—it was best that she be honest with him. "Danny, these rugs won't stay with us. I'm going to sell them. We need the money to buy seeds for that garden you've been dreaming of." When

Danny's chin fell in disappointment, she added, "Don't be upset, Danny. This is going to be a grand year for us, you'll see." She really believed it was true, and Danny could see the hope shining in her once dim eyes.

Then Danny did something he'd never done before. He leaned over and hugged his old Aunt Winnie. She stiffened in surprise. *How long had it been since someone had really cared for her?* she wondered. It was a strange and wonderful feeling.

Winnie patted Danny on the back hesitantly and cleared her throat to stifle the tears of joy that were welling up inside her. "You go on out now. Try to stay clean and be good." She was surprised to hear a quiver in her voice.

CHAPTER 10

Hatching Dreams

The following day Doris hurriedly completed her chores and then ran up the hill to the apple tree where she and Danny had agreed to meet. She had figured out how she could help Danny and his aunt, and she couldn't wait to tell him.

Danny was already sitting under the tree, dreaming of all the apples that it would hold in the fall. He didn't even see Doris coming.

"Hi, Danny," Doris called out as she approached the tree. "Hey, that wool shirt looks real nice on you. I'll bet you're a lot warmer now, huh?" She handed him a small bundle filled with potatoes, then smiled nervously.

"Potatoes! Thanks. You bet I'm warmer!" He stood up, grinning from ear to ear. "Hey, what's in the basket?"

"I brought you a present. But you have to promise to do everything just the way I tell you to, okay?" she warned.

"Okay, sure. What is it?"

"Eggs...but not to eat. I got them from one of our hens. They are due to hatch in a couple of days. I've wrapped them up real good to keep them warm. But you need to take them home now and keep them wrapped up and by the fire, or else they won't hatch."

Doris looked at Danny's excited expression and realized he had no idea how important this could be for him. "Danny, this isn't just about having some cute pet chickens running around. If I had brought you just one fresh egg, you would go home and eat it and it would be gone. This is different. I am giving you an endless supply of eggs. Do you see how important it is that you take care of them? I doubt I'll be able to get you any more if this doesn't work."

Danny did see, and he was more grateful than he could ever express. "Are you going to get in trouble for this, Doris? Because I don't want them if you are going to get in trouble." Danny meant it. He'd come to realize just how important having friends was.

"It's okay, Danny, no one will miss these four eggs—I don't think. You'll have to make a little chicken house and a pen for them after they've hatched. Your aunt will know how to care for them. You should go now and get them by a fire. Carry them home under your shirt next to your body to keep them warm. I've got to go, but I'll meet you out here tomorrow after chores—at around five o'clock. Bye, Danny." Doris turned and started down the hill.

Danny stood for a moment with the precious bundle in his hands. He wondered why Doris was trying so hard to help him. Why would she give so much, even risking getting into trouble? He knew that they'd be friends forever, and he was determined to pay her back somehow, someday.

"Doris?" he called out as she bounded down the hill.

She stopped and turned to face him, smiling. "Yes?"

"What's your surname? Aunt Winnie was wondering who your family was," he asked a little nervously. It was strange to be asking her this now when he already felt like he had known her forever.

"Free," Doris stated proudly. "Doris Free."

"Doris Free. That's just about the finest name I've ever heard," Danny said admiringly. Then, before Doris could ask him his surname in return, Danny turned, and with light steps, started making his way home.

He couldn't wait to show Winnie the precious gift. He would guard the chicks and raise them with love until he and Winnie had their own thriving farm. So certain was Danny of this happening that it was almost as if he expected cows and horses as well as chickens to hatch from the four eggs. As a matter of fact, it wasn't far from the truth. Doris's acts of kindness would indeed grow and hatch into something bigger and more wonderful for her poor neighbors. Life would never be the same for them.

Winnie wiped tears of joy from her eyes as she watched Danny carefully remove the eggs from his shirt while explaining where they had come from. He placed the eggs into a basket by the stove. It seemed too good to be true, and for a moment Winnie couldn't think clearly. But then her practical side took over, and she sprang into action. "If I don't pull myself together, we won't have any chicks at all to be excited about. I'll wrap these eggs, and you run outside and find two large flat rocks. We will have to keep a warm rock under them until they hatch."

Danny quickly found two rocks that would fit nicely in the bottom of the basket. After prying them out of the still partially frozen ground, he went back inside and rinsed them off in the sink basin. Any other time, washing rocks in the kitchen basin would certainly have been forbidden.

Winnie placed the rocks in the wood stove to warm them. She and Danny began making out a schedule that would keep one of them in charge of the eggs at all times until they hatched. It would mean both of them losing some sleep, but neither of them minded when they thought of the little chicks they would soon have. They spent the rest of the day planning the chicken house that they would build.

Danny's eyes were glowing with excitement, and Winnie, too, was as giddy as a girl while they planned out their rosier-looking future. She would have been embarrassed if she could have seen how flushed her cheeks were. What a difference one kind, young girl had made in their lives!

The next few days were the happiest that Winnie and Danny had known since the death of Danny's parents. The weather continued to warm up and feel more like springtime, and before long they became the proud parents of four fuzzy yellow chicks.

CHAPTER 11

New Additions

Doris took the last of the day's wash down off the clothesline and folded it into the basket. The sun was setting, and the air was turning cool, so she wanted to get back into the house.

Ma had sent Arla out to help Doris with the laundry, but instead Arla was twirling around in circles and giggling as her hair flew wildly around her face. Arla never could stick to one task for long. She just bounced happily from activity to activity, rarely accomplishing much at all it seemed.

"Arla, you carry this basket of clothes to the porch. I've got to go and tie up Tippy before we go in," Doris directed her sister. But Arla just kept spinning around and around. "Arla!" Doris shouted and grabbed her sister's shoulders, pointing her swaying body toward the wicker basket. "The basket of clothes."

Doris let go, and Arla walked a zigzag path over to the basket and picked it up with a silly grin. "Got it!" she exclaimed triumphantly, as though she had just accomplished a major feat.

"Don't forget the bag of clothespins off the line. Ma

doesn't like them to be left out overnight," Doris said over her shoulder on her way to the barn.

The stray pup was still hanging around the farm, but Doris made sure she was tied up every night. The girls had started calling her Tippy, because the tip of her tail was white while the rest of her was light brown. They knew that Pa would make them get rid of the pup once they had found her a good home, but they were enjoying Tippy while they had her.

By the time Doris returned to the house, Victoria, Jena, and Ma had finished cooking supper, and Pa was already washed up and seated at the table, reading his new *Farmer's Almanac*. Doris was hungry. It seemed like everyone got a little hungrier once the weather started warming up and they began spending more time outside. Ma had made chicken hash using canned chicken—Doris's favorite. She breathed deeply as she washed her hands, savoring the salty smell, then sat down at the table.

The girls chatted about school and their friends while passing the chicken hash and fried squash around the table. As they ate, Pa turned the talk to the spring planting and the extra help he would need from the girls. It was a busy time of year on the farm, but the whole family looked forward to the activity after the long cold winter. A couple of calves and a colt would be born shortly, and all of the chicks would soon hatch. Doris hoped that Pa wouldn't notice that there were four fewer chicks than he had planned for.

Ma was the only one who noticed that Doris was being especially quiet. She seemed deep in thought and wasn't eating as much as usual. Doris was always the one who got the most excited about the new animals that would soon be born on the farm, but tonight she hadn't said a word about it. Ma figured Doris was upset about the stray dog, Tippy. Doris had always been sensitive, especially when it came to animals. Ma was sure she would pull out of it soon.

Then Pa made an announcement. "Girls, I have made a deal with one of our neighbors. I was going to save it for a surprise, but it looks like I may need your help to prepare for it, so I'll just have to tell you now." He looked at each girl's face as they stared at him, eyes wide with excitement. He paused, wanting to make them wait so that the surprise would be even sweeter, but Arla couldn't stand the suspense.

"What is it, Pa? What is it? What is it?" she begged. Arla sounded as if she was in actual pain.

"Okay," Pa said, chuckling at his youngest, "I'll tell you, but you have to promise you'll help me get ready for it." He looked at them with mock sternness.

The girls all nodded and promised they would help if he would just tell them what the surprise was. Even Doris was now paying attention.

"Well, you see, your mother has agreed to make a quilt top for the Thompsons. If you recall, their oldest daughter is getting married in the fall, and . . ." Jena groaned at the long explanation and Arla wiggled fitfully in her chair, twisting her face in agony over her father's attempt to drag out his surprise. "Okay, okay. . . the Thompsons are going to give us two little lambs in exchange—"

"Two *real* little lambs?" Arla squealed, jumping out of her chair and spinning in a circle all in one motion. "Can one of them sleep with me? What do lambs eat anyhow? Can we give them names? How big will they be? Are they white?"

Everyone laughed at Arla's high spirits and breathless questions. "It sounds like you have a lot to learn about our new additions to the farm!" Ma declared, shaking her finger at Arla and laughing. "When I was a child, we had sheep, and it was my job to spin the wool into yarn after my pa sheared them each spring. It will be a little while before we have enough wool to make yarn, but just think of the warm things we'll be able to make from the wool! We can knit socks, mittens, and hats. When I was about Arla's age, my grandmother knit me a sweater from a black sheep's wool. Well, I thought I was the luckiest girl in the world to have all of that wool just for me. I wore that sweater until it was so tight that I could hardly breathe." Ma sighed, and a faraway look came into her eyes as she enjoyed her memories.

Pa laid his hand on top of Ma's as he continued the sheep lesson. "A young lamb needs a lot of looking after. You know how sheep always have shepherds watching over them?" The girls nodded and waited to hear more. "Well, that's because they will wander off and could get hurt or eaten by a wolf if someone isn't there to protect them. We'll have to fix a section of the barn to keep them in—probably where we keep the feed, saddles, and harnesses. Then I'll build a shed off the side of the barn for the feed and supplies.

"We already have much to do this spring, and your mother will need some extra help with the piecing of the quilt, too. I think we are about to have the busiest spring ever, but it will be worth it. We are lucky to have such a problem during these hard times. Most people would love to have so much good fortune that they can hardly keep up with all of the work. You girls have helped to make all of this possible. Some of the clothes that you found in the dump will go into the wedding quilt that we will trade for the lambs."

The girls were proud that they had helped their family. They smiled at one another. It was quiet in the room just then, and everyone felt happy to be part of the family. Doris was joyful for a moment, but then she thought about Danny and his aunt and how they must be cold and hungry tonight. With no family and no farm, their future wasn't looking as bright and promising as the Frees'.

Doris didn't yet realize how much Danny's and his aunt's lives had already improved due to her small acts of kindness. Later that evening, while Doris was falling asleep feeling sad for Danny and Aunt Winnie, they were going to bed feeling quite fortunate and happy. The compassion of one little girl had changed the world after all . . . and she had no idea just how much she had set into motion.

CHAPTER 12

Difficult Decisions

The next few days were rainy and cool. The girls knew that the rain was needed to get the soil ready for the crops that they would soon plant, but they still wished for it to end. They were all anxious to get outside and start preparing a place for the lambs that would soon be arriving.

Pa worked hard building a pen in the barn for the sheep. He moved the feed and supplies out of the way, but wouldn't be able to build the storage shed until the rain stopped. The girls wanted to help him, but he insisted that they work on the quilt top instead. They needed to get a good start on the quilt while it rained, because once the weather cleared up, work on the farm would double.

Doris was disappointed because she hadn't been able to meet Danny due to the bad weather. She wondered if all the eggs she'd given him had hatched, and she was worried about how he would find food in the rain. It would be easier for him in the summer when there would be wild berries, roots, and more animals around. But then the harsh winter would come again. *There must be a way to help Danny and his aunt find a permanent way to care for themselves,* thought Doris. It seemed an impossible task for one girl to accomplish.

Victoria and Jena used the stiff templates Ma had made for a quilt pattern and cut out the shapes that would make the wedding band quilt for the Thompsons' daughter. Ma had drawn a picture of the quilt and labeled what colors she wanted the pieces to be. They would have just enough fabric to finish, so it was important that they not make any mistakes when cutting out the pieces.

Doris was good at pinning all of the pieces together. She laid them out on a little wooden table next to Ma's sewing machine when she was finished. Ma was proud of her treadle sewing machine, and it certainly made the piecework go faster than if they had to sew it by hand. The girls would all help with the hand stitching around each piece after the squares were sewn together. Ma was a good quilt maker, but she would work hard to earn the two lambs. The Thompsons would be pleased with this quilt.

Everyone was unusually quiet while they worked. Most of the time they talked while they sewed, and Doris liked to make up her exotic stories. But today they were concentrating extra hard because they wanted to finish the quilt as quickly as possible. Arla got bored and tried to get Doris started on a story, but Doris said she needed to concentrate on pinning the pieces together evenly, and telling one of her stories would distract her.

In truth, Doris was too caught up thinking about Danny and Winnie to make up a story. She still hadn't come up with a way to help them without giving away things that her own family needed. She really hated

keeping secrets from her family.

Arla spent her time cutting up the clothes that were the most worn. She cut long strips in the same way that Danny's aunt had, by cutting spirals up the sleeves then zigzags across the back. She tried to make each strip of fabric as long as possible. When she had several long pieces cut, Ma would set aside the quilt square she was working on, sew the strips together, and then Arla could wind them into a large ball. They would be able to make several rugs out of the rags the girls had found.

By the end of the week, they had a large portion of the quilt pieced together, and Arla had all of the rags cut up and rolled into three big balls. Each ball would make a rug. Pa had completed the sheep pen in the barn and had drawn out the plans for the storage shed, which he would begin building the following week.

Late Friday night Pa announced that he had talked to Mr. Thompson and that the lambs would be delivered in a week. He also informed his family that the planting was to begin in two weeks. The girls would be expected to prepare the garden while Ma continued to work on the quilt. She had already completed one rug and had traded it in town for seeds they needed for the vegetable garden.

That gave Doris an idea. One way that she could help Danny would be to give him some seeds so he could plant a garden. That would give them food to eat this fall, and then they could save some of it to help them get through the winter. She doubted that she could give him enough to have a big garden this year, though. Her own family needed the seeds badly. That winter they'd had to eat some of the bean seeds that were intended for the garden.

Doris was so confused. She knew that helping her neighbors was the right thing to do, but she felt like she was stealing from her own family to do it, and she knew that wasn't right. Everything was so complicated, and she couldn't sort it all out.

Somehow Doris was going to have to find a way to talk to her parents about Danny and Winnie, but how could she do that without betraying her new friends? She knew that Winnie didn't want anyone involved in her business. Doris wanted to find a way to bring them all together so they could help one another the way that neighbors were supposed to. She shoved a few stray pieces of hair behind her right ear in frustration.

CHAPTER 13

Chicks and Lambs

Over the weekend the weather cleared. On Saturday afternoon Danny and Doris met under the apple tree. Doris told Danny all about the little lambs they were preparing for and how they would all help to take care of them.

Danny had a grin from ear to ear as he told Doris about the chicks that had hatched and how they were eating every wiggly thing they could find. He and his aunt were keeping them in the house for now in a makeshift pen until they were big enough to be safe outside. Danny worried about the foxes that were in the woods and wished that he had a dog to protect his chickens.

"I'm building a chicken house for them, Doris. Winnie drew out how to make a sturdy frame, and I figured out how to make a little door that I can close at night to keep them safe. I've been looking at the dump for some more wood to finish it. The chicks are growing real fast. When the weather is warmer, they'll love being outside."

Danny was proud of his baby chickens and of the house he was building for them. He was also happy about the changes he'd been seeing in his aunt. "Winnie is getting a garden spot ready. She says this rain makes the ground just right for starting a garden." He looked at Doris and was quiet for a moment. "You know, Doris, Winnie is different now with those little chicks running around. She laughs and smiles now. I don't think I'd ever heard her laugh for real until those eggs came into our house. She even gave me a hug the other day. I think those eggs were magical, Doris." Danny looked dreamily at the puffy clouds overhead and continued in almost a whisper. "Yes, indeed, magical eggs that made the dream of having a real farm come true."

Doris giggled at the thought of magical eggs, but Danny continued on so seriously that she quickly stopped.

"Aunt Winnie used to be real angry inside, and she never talked to anyone. But she wove a nice rug out of the rags I found at the dump—she has this big loom in the basement and she can make a rug really fast—and then she took it to town and traded it for some seeds. She said we still need more seeds so we'll be able to store some food for the winter, but that it's a start. When she went to town, she talked to the man at the store and even smiled when he told her how nice the rug was. I could tell he was surprised that she wasn't mean and angry." The words came tumbling out with barely a pause.

For the first time, Doris realized that she had already given Danny and Winnie something very important: hope. Hope for a better life and hope that there was still good in the world. It felt wonderful to see how her actions helped these good people, but still Doris worried about all the secrets she was keeping. She wondered how her family would react if they found out what she had done.

She also worried that Danny and Winnie were expecting too much. Sure they would have a few eggs and a small garden, but that was still a long way from having an actual farm and the money to buy all the things they really needed. Doris knew that she wouldn't be able to get her hands on the items that had been taken from Winnie, and she worried that when her new friends realized how unattainable their dream still was, they'd get discouraged and give up altogether. She couldn't bear that.

CHAPTER 14

Winnie

Doris visited Winnie and Danny whenever she could get away without being missed. At first Aunt Winnie kept quiet with a watchful, suspicious look on her pale face. Her brown hair flecked with gray was always pulled back into a tight bun, making her look stern. It wasn't long until she warmed up to Doris, though. She watched the way her nephew laughed around his new friend as they played with the chicks, and she was grateful.

The farm and the house still needed a lot of work. Doris suspected that little had been done since Winnie's husband had died. Danny was determined to clean and fix everything, and he'd already begun clearing away the weeds and junk that had piled up over the years. Doris admired his determination. Danny reminded Doris of her father in some ways. No matter how difficult a task was, her pa would chip away at it until it was done. Danny was doing the same with the farm—fixing it up little by little. Doris no longer doubted that Danny and Winnie would have a real farm of their own someday. She knew Danny would make his dream real.

Winnie showed Doris her big loom in the basement

and how she used it to weave the rag balls into rugs. Doris was fascinated by the dozens of strings pulled tight across the surface of the loom and the magical way the rags were transformed into a colorful rug as they moved through the strings. She wondered if her father knew how to build a loom like this. She'd love to learn how to weave such beautiful patterns.

Eventually, Doris and Winnie became comfortable with each other. One day, after watching Winnie weave for a while, Doris began one of her stories about who might have worn the rags when they were still beautiful clothes. She described a railroad man with four children and no wife. "He worked hard to keep a roof over his children's heads, to make sure they had plenty of food, and to buy them nice clothes to wear to school."

Doris stared out the window and continued weaving her story at the same time that Winnie wove the rug together. "The children, however, made things difficult for their father because they loved animals so much that they brought home every stray they found. The father was tired of coming home to a house full of noisy pigs, goats, geese, frogs, and whatever else the children had found, so one day he punished them. He refused to buy them any new clothes until they got rid of all the animals. Well, that was simple; the children figured, what did they need new clothes for? So they kept their pets and just wore their old clothes until they were tattered rags. Finally, their father gave in. He bought them some new clothes and threw the rags into the dump."

"Their father also realized how good his children were with animals. Shortly thereafter they started up a business

taking care of other people's animals while the owners were out of town or if they were sick. The children loved it, and it meant their father didn't have to work on the railroad anymore. The whole family was happy because they were able to spend more time together. The end."

Doris fell silent. She had never told one of her stories to anyone besides family, and she was more than a little anxious that Danny and Winnie would think it was dumb. But Winnie and Danny were smiling. "Why, child, I believe you have the gift of storytelling. That was absolutely wonderful!" Winnie praised, breaking the awkward silence. "Do you ever write any of your stories down?"

Doris shook her head. It had never occurred to her to write them down—she just made them up as she went along to entertain her family while they sewed.

"Well, you should. You could write a whole book of stories and sell them. People would like to read stories like that, I reckon. A gift like yours is meant to be shared, child. Don't you forget that now, okay?" Winnie looked at Doris, waiting for the girl's promise.

Doris wiggled in her seat nervously. "Okay, I guess I could write some of them down. Usually, I make up new ones each time, but there are some that my sisters like so much that they make me tell them over and over. I bet I could write those out pretty fast. I don't know if anyone else would want to read them, though."

"Well, you write them and we'll see about that," Winnie replied with the spunk of a much younger woman. Her newfound hope for a brighter future filled her heart with a warm glow.

"You know, Doris, my father built me this loom many

years ago. I still have a copy of the pattern he used. If your pa might want to build one for your family, I believe I could help him. I watched every step my father took in building this one, and I know every inch of it by heart."

"Really?" Doris asked, her eyes so big and round with excitement that Winnie couldn't help but laugh. The older woman was amazed by the joy her nephew and his sweet friend had brought to her life. Something else surprised her even more, though. Winnie had begun thinking about spending time with other people. Maybe it was finally time for her to rejoin her community.

Doris babbled excitedly. "I'll ask Pa. This is a busy time what with planting season and the new lambs coming this week, so I'm not sure he'd have time to work on something like that now. But he is real handy, and I know he'd be able to make a fine loom. Maybe this winter when he has more time. When we went to town earlier this week, Ma stopped by Mr. Shutter's store and was admiring that rug you sold to him. I could tell that she liked it a lot and wished that she could have it. It was that blue and yellow one. Wouldn't it be something if she could make a rug like that for herself!" Doris finished wistfully.

"Well, it took me a while to catch on, but I had a good teacher in my mother. With some lessons and lots of practice, I'm sure that your ma could make something even nicer. When I had more money for yarn and wool, I used to weave fine fabric for blankets and suit coats. I kept my own sheep for wool. I'm not sure these old hands are suited to fine fabrics anymore, but they work just fine for rag rugs." Winnie held her hands up to the light and flexed them.

Doris noticed that the woman looked much younger when she smiled. In fact, these days Winnie always seemed younger than she did when they'd first met. At first she seemed like an old woman, but now it was clear that she was still full of life. It couldn't be the coming of spring alone that caused this dramatic change, could it? Doris suspected there was much more to it than that.

CHAPTER 15

Secrets
Revealed

As the weeks passed, the days got longer and warmer. Buds began to open on the trees, animals awakened from their winter sleep, and birds that had gone south for the winter were home again and searching for nesting materials. Arla piled pieces of string and fabric out by the clothesline for the birds. The girls did this every spring and were always delighted to spot a nest high in a tree with a recognizable pattern of fabric peeking through it.

Pa started building the small shed alongside the barn. He put up large shelves to stack the grain sacks on so the mice couldn't get to them and also so the moisture from the ground wouldn't ruin it. Pa put in a half door, which would prevent the sheep from wandering in and eating the grain. A small hole in the door allowed the cats in so they could rid the shed of mice.

Arla thought the cat door was the best idea in the whole world. Pa was always coming up with ways to improve things. He tinkered with every tool he bought, changing and improving them all. Ma used to get mad that he changed things they'd spent good money for, but she eventually realized that the tools and appliances worked better after he was done with them. His girls were certain that he was the smartest man in the whole county.

Jena and Victoria helped Ma with the spring cleaning while Doris finished sewing the details onto the quilt. It was almost done and would be ready when the sheep were delivered. Arla pestered everyone about the lambs, asking several times a day why they couldn't be brought sooner. Ma explained that they weren't ready to be away from their mother's milk yet, but Arla didn't think this was a good enough reason. Jena decided that they all couldn't wait for the lambs to arrive more because they wanted Arla to shut up than because they wanted the lambs that much. Arla could try a person's nerves.

Ma was just happy to see the warm weather arrive because it meant the planting season was coming. She had already planted seedlings in trays on the windowsills that she would then replant in the garden once it was plowed. This would give the plants a head start. Ma was still worried, though, because they had so little food left, and it would be a long time until these seeds would grow into anything harvestable.

The girls would have to gather the edible spring plants that grew wild on the farm and they would have to make do until the garden started to ripen. Ma hoped for a good growing season, so they would have a better store of food to last them through next winter and spring. The previous year had been too dry for a really good harvest.

This year will be better, I know it will, thought Ma. It just felt like a year of hopes fulfilled and dreams come true. They would have sheep of their own, and this time next spring, they would be shearing them and spinning the wool into yarn. Ma smiled as she remembered the dream she'd had the night before in which she had been half-buried in balls of different-colored wool. The good fortune that had befallen them made her optimistic about her family's future.

The girls started getting restless despite all the extra work they had to do after school. In some ways this was the hardest time of year—more difficult to get through even than the dead of winter. This was because everyone knew spring was just around the corner; they could smell it in the air, and yet the mornings and evenings were still too cold to really enjoy being outside. The girls itched for the carefree days of summer.

Ma noticed that Doris was especially restless, more so even than hyperactive Arla. She tried to talk to her daughter about it one day, but Doris just said she was fine and nothing more. Doris couldn't be bothered with conversation—she had more important things on her mind. Whenever Ma asked her a question, Doris would give the shortest answer possible, then go back to whatever she'd been doing as though she hated to be interrupted. Doris knew she would feel better if she talked about what was weighing on her mind. But that would mean explaining everything that had happened, and she didn't want to get Danny or Winnie into trouble (or herself, for that matter). So instead she kept it a secret and became more and more withdrawn.

Danny had asked Doris if he could borrow some gardening tools. Winnie didn't even have a shovel, so Danny had been using scrap metal to dig through the dirt to prepare it for seeds. Doris wanted to help, but she wasn't sure she could get the tools to Danny without anyone noticing. Even if she did manage to get them off the farm without anyone seeing, what if her pa went looking for a tool and it wasn't there? Doris didn't think her family would understand her befriending a woman whom no one liked and a boy who didn't go to school or have shoes. She figured there must be a good reason why her family had ignored their neighbor for this long and that they wouldn't be happy about Doris helping them.

Tonight Doris sat on the sofa with her sewing, thinking. Arla had fallen asleep right after supper and had to be carried upstairs to bed. Pa had gone back out to the barn to put the finishing touches on the gate for the new sheep pen. Jena and Victoria were outside doing some last-minute chores, and Ma was darning socks. It was a quiet evening.

Suddenly the front door clattered open, and Jena and Victoria came in noisily, chattering away. Doris, caught up in her thoughts, was so startled by the sudden commotion that she jumped.

"He can't take Tippy, Victoria—he is mean to everything. You know that he cut the tail off the last pup he had," Jena said, almost pleading with her sister.

"Jena, we've tried every neighbor and everyone at school. No one else is willing to take a puppy right now. After all, that little thing won't ever grow big enough to help in a hunt or to herd the cows. All she'll be is a pet, and no one has extra food for a pet right now." Victoria didn't want the class bully, Foot Zimmer, to take the pup either, but his parents were the only ones willing to even consider it.

For days Doris had been mulling over the best way to bring up the issue of Danny and Tippy. Suddenly it was now or never. Doris tried to hide her shaking hands under her sewing as she said as calmly as possible, "I've already found someone to take Tippy." The words came out too rushed to sound as casual as she had hoped.

Ma and the girls turned to Doris with interest. Doris looked down at her sewing, took a deep breath, and continued. "He's kind and would never hurt Tippy. I know that he'll take care of her real well and would even give the pup his own food if he had to. He wants a dog more than anything in the world."

"Who's this person, Doris?" asked Jena, posing the question that was on everyone's mind.

Without meeting anyone's eyes, Doris began trying to explain. She wished she had rehearsed what she was going to say. "You know Miss Winnie who lives over the hill?"

"You don't mean to give the pup to that witch lady, do you?" Victoria interrupted, "She might boil her and eat her!"

Ma tried to hide her smile and pretended to be shocked. "Victoria, that is the most ridiculous thing I've ever heard." She continued sternly, "Why, you don't even know Winnie. This family does not sink to the habit of listening to the vicious rumors spread by ignorant people." Ma caught her breath and looked at Doris. "Now, Doris, you said it was a boy who wanted the pup. Who is this boy and what does he have to do with Winnie Stephens?"

"Well, Winnie has a nephew who's been staying with her for about a year. His name is Danny, and he really would like Tippy for his own. He's working hard to turn that overgrown land into a real farm and to make that shack into a nice home. He would take good care of him and so would Miss Winnie. She really isn't mean at all. She loves animals. And you should see how she makes rugs with this big loom. She . . ." Doris realized she'd said much more than she'd intended to, but she continued anyway. "Danny will take care of Tippy. He lost his parents, and he needs to have something to love. Something besides Winnie, that is." She was almost pleading now.

Victoria tilted her head and looked suspiciously at Doris. "If this boy has been here for a year already, why isn't he in school? How old is he anyhow?"

"He's nine, and he doesn't go to school. Winnie won't let him. She remembers how mean everyone in town was to her, and she figures the kids at school will be just as nasty to Danny. Things have been tough for him, what with losing his parents and all. Winnie is real good to him. They don't have much, though. They went hungry a lot this past winter."

Ma shook her head and made a sympathetic clucking sound. "I don't blame her for feeling the way she does about the townsfolk. People were awful to her when her husband died, and no one has ever made right by her. Everyone seems to think that if they pretend nothing happened, then they didn't actually do anything wrong. Since she rarely comes to town, they aren't reminded of their bad behavior. I think it's about time for Winnie to become part of this town again. Maybe this nephew of hers will be just the thing to bring her around."

"He's a nice boy, and I can tell Winnie loves him . . . in her own way," Doris told her mother.

Ma sighed as she tried to absorb everything Doris had just told them. "Doris, I want to meet this boy before we give him the pup, but I'm sure it will be just fine. Later I want to hear about how you came to know so much about Winnie and her nephew when none of us have even seen the boy! But now it's time for bed."

"And all of you don't forget to clean your teeth and brush your hair before bed," she added as the girls walked up the stairs, whispering to each other. They would have a lot to talk about while they rubbed the thin gauze over their teeth and brushed each other's hair.

When Pa came in, Ma filled him in on the evening's excitement and then sat quietly in front of the stove for a long while, thinking about all that Doris had told her. She was sure there was a lot more to the story. Doris had always been a quiet, thoughtful girl who cared greatly about other people. She had done the Free family proud by ignoring the rumors and befriending Winnie and her nephew.

Ma and Pa talked late into the night, wondering how so much could have happened right under their noses without them even noticing.

CHAPTER 16

Changes

It was that time of year when days passed quickly, what with all the planting, hoeing, and other farmwork that had to be done. The girls had enjoyed the end-of-the-year program they put on at school, but they were more excited about the last day of school. Victoria said she would miss her friends, but the other girls were thrilled to be free of lessons and homework. They were certain it was going to be the greatest summer ever.

Doris had told her parents everything about Danny: when and where she first met him, the hard times he'd been through, and the various ways she'd tried to help him, including the eggs she'd secretly given to him. Doris was relieved when Ma and Pa said they weren't angry with her. But when they told her it was shame that she didn't tell them everything right away because then they could have done even more to help, Doris felt a pang of guilt.

More than a week passed before Doris saw Danny and Winnie again and was able to bring up meeting her family. Ma had suggested that they all get together for a picnic, but Doris knew how Winnie felt about strangers, and she doubted the older woman would agree to it.

Pa had agreed to lend Danny a hoe so he could break up the soil and prepare the garden for planting. Now Doris walked slowly over the hill on her way to Danny and Winnie's house, dragging the hoe behind her and carving a groove in the dirt. Usually she scampered over the hill, anxious to see her friends, but today she was so nervous about what Winnie would think of the picnic idea that she didn't want the walk to end.

When she finally got to the top of the hill and looked down on the old Stephens place, she hardly recognized it. The ivy and brush had been completely cleared away from the house, there was a stone path leading to the front door, and more of the garden soil had been turned over. The garden still wasn't completely broken up due to their lack of tools, and Doris knew that if they didn't plant soon, there wouldn't be enough time for a garden to grow. The hoe would help, but Doris didn't think there was any way one boy could do all the work necessary to plant a decent-sized garden.

Then Doris noticed Danny at the side of the house. He was painting the shutters a bright, cheery yellow. He turned and saw Doris, waved, and laid down the paint-brush. Winnie was out by the chicken coop talking to the growing chicks while she scattered seed for them. Most of the day they roamed free, eating whatever insects they could find because there wasn't much money for chicken feed. But now and again, Winnie treated them.

Doris realized it was the first time she had ever seen Winnie outside the house. The woman still wasn't what you could call sprightly, but she was no longer the frail, old-looking woman Doris had first met. She seemed to be

getting healthier and hardier as the days passed. Seeing Danny and Winnie working together and caring for the farm as a team lifted Doris's spirits. She happily trotted the rest of the way down the hill to meet them.

"Hey, Doris," shouted Danny, "what do you think of the house? Aunt Winnie said she hadn't seen the whole thing in so long that she had forgotten what it looked like!" He beamed with pride over the hard work he had done. Winnie shook her head and smiled. For years the little house had been hidden, as if in shame, under thick ivy. But now, after many years of not caring at all, Winnie was once again proud of her little house.

"How about this paint!" Winnie added with real emotion. "Someone ordered it from Mr. Shutter at the Dime Store by accident, so he was happy to get rid of it for nothing. Isn't it the most wonderful color you have ever seen? I've always wanted to have a bright and cheery house, but I could never afford the paint. I know this will only do the shutters, but someday we'll paint the whole house, won't we, Danny?"

It said a lot that Winnie was planning a future for her and Danny. She had hope again and was no longer sad. However, Doris wondered if the change in Winnie included forgiving the townsfolk and if she would let them back into her life. Doris hoped so, for Danny's sake. It was the only way his life would ever start to feel normal again.

Winnie smiled and gestured to the neat, narrow path leading up to the front door. She and Danny had made it from smooth pebbles they'd gathered from the creek. "I'm going out to the field to look for some flowers to dig up and replant along the path. I remember seeing some lily of the valley, which should grow nicely in this shady spot here. Would you like to tag along, Doris?"

Doris held up the hoe. "I brought this for you to borrow. I could hoe a row alongside the path while you get the flowers, and then it will be ready for planting when you get back."

"That would be wonderful, child. I won't be long— the flowers are just on the edge of the forest. There was once a house there years ago, and flowers still grow in what used to be the front yard," she said, gesturing vaguely toward the trees. Then she was on her way.

Danny finished rinsing his paintbrush with turpentine and stood back to admire the house with Doris. In actuality, the wood siding was a dingy gray with only flecks of paint left here and there, so the gleaming yellow shutters were a little shocking and out of place. But the children thought it shone like a castle.

"You sure have done a lot of work here, Danny. I hardly recognized the house when I came over the hill," said Doris with a sincere smile. "You'll have to get to work on that garden, though, or it will be too late to plant. The house can wait until after the seedlings have sprouted. Other farmers have just about all of their crops planted already, and Ma said that the ladies in her quilting circle have begun planting their gardens, too."

Danny looked at the small patch of earth that he had been able to chop up so far with the pieces of metal that he found at the dump. "It sure is a lot of work. I don't know if I can get it all done in time. I bet all of those ladies with their fancy gardens had a tractor or at least a horse to pull and till. I've only got my two hands, and I've been out here digging 'til they are bleeding from the rough metal I've been scooping with. That hoe you brought will help out a whole lot. You won't get in trouble for bringing it, will you?" He looked at Doris with worry in his eyes.

"No, I won't get into trouble. I'm glad I can help." Doris started hoeing a row next to the path. The soil was packed down hard, and the work was more difficult than she had expected. Doris was used to her mother's garden, which was soft from years of planting and weeding. It would indeed be difficult for Danny to plant in such hard soil. But the soil was rich and black and would grow a fine garden once it was tilled.

Doris was trying to think of a way to ask Danny about meeting her family; the roundabout way that she had planned seemed silly now. Doris decided the direct route would be best. "Danny, I told my family about you and Winnie, and about how I've been helping you and how hard you're working. I told them about you not having enough to eat. They all want to meet you, Danny, and they want Winnie to be part of this town again. . . ."

The words came out in a rush and then Doris trailed off nervously as Danny began eyeing her suspiciously. He had been with Winnie long enough for some of her mistrust of others to rub off on him. He knew he could trust Doris, but the rest of her family was another matter. And here she was talking about the whole town!

"Now what did you go and do something like that for, Doris? Winnie and I are doing just fine, and we don't need anyone meddling in our business. I don't want anyone feeling sorry for us—we're happy and have a good home." Danny was confused. He wasn't really angry, just scared.

He felt safe here with Winnie, and it made him nervous to think about other people entering their lives and causing things to change. Maybe they would change for the better, but Danny didn't want to take that chance.

Doris was hoeing faster and harder now—Danny had hurt her feelings. He felt bad about it. Doris was a good friend, and he knew she was just trying to help. He couldn't blame her for not wanting to keep this secret from her family any longer.

"I'm sorry, Doris. I'm not angry, honest. I'm just surprised, that's all," Danny apologized. His large brown eyes were wide and sincere. "So your parents said that we could use this hoe, then?"

Doris nodded, not trusting her voice.

"That was nice of them," Danny continued. "Thank them for us. We'll return it as soon as we can. I'll be real careful with it, and I'll even oil the handle before I give it back."

Doris leaned on the hoe. Feeling like she could trust her voice again, she finished what she had come over to say in the first place. "My ma and pa want you and Winnie to come to a picnic at our house this weekend. Ma makes the best fried chicken, and we even have oranges to make some orangeade. Victoria is going to use the last of the sugar to bake a cake, and we have some preserves to put on top of it. It will be a wonderful picnic, Danny, and no one else in town will be there."

Thinking that Danny might need some extra convincing, she added, "Ma says that if we are going to give you Tippy, then she needs to meet you first." Doris continued hoeing, but saw out of the corner of her eye that Danny's face lit up with the mention of the pup. She knew then that she had won him over. That just left Winnie.

When Danny spoke again, he had completely changed his tune. "Well, Doris, a picnic sure does sound fun. Winnie will be hard to convince, though. We'll have to be careful about how we bring it up to her. She does have good things to say about your folks, though—likes them better than she does most people around here. When my uncle died, your folks brought Winnie a meal once, and they never took anything from her even though my uncle owed your pa some money. Everyone else in town took whatever they could. Even though she thinks your parents are good people, I'm still not sure she'll agree to a picnic, though."

Danny took a breath, thought for a minute, and continued. "Hmm . . . I have an idea. Let me think on it while I put these painting supplies away. You finish that row for the flowers. Winnie will be back soon."

A few minutes later, they saw Winnie walking back. Danny motioned Doris to be silent about the picnic. Winnie didn't say much, but she was humming the song "Happy Days Are Here Again" to herself. Sprigs of lily of the valley filled the homemade basket she had woven from cattail reeds.

Winnie spent the next few hours planting the flowers while Doris and Danny took turns hoeing the hard sod. They decided to prepare just a few rows at a time rather than making a square for the entire plot all at once. This way Danny could begin planting a few things right away and then continue adding rows to the garden one at a time, planting the fastest-growing plants last.

They made good progress that afternoon. By the time Doris was heading home, Danny was already planting the first two rows of the garden while Winnie pumped water to soak the newly planted seedlings. Before she left, Danny whispered to Doris that he'd let her know about the picnic the next day.

Doris hoped with all her heart that Winnie accepted the invitation. If Winnie refused, then there was little more Doris could do to help her, though she knew she'd keep trying. But if Winnie agreed to the picnic, then things were going to change for the whole town. Doris was hopeful, but she couldn't help worrying about what would happen if Winnie accepted the invitation, they all met, and then things went badly. Then her parents might not want her to be friends with Danny and Winnie anymore. Doris knew she would have trouble sleeping that night, awaiting the arrival of the next day and Danny's answer.

CHAPTER 17

Planning a Picnic

The next afternoon Danny came by to tell Doris that he and Winnie would be at the picnic. Doris was thrilled. Pa was outside working on a broken section of the plow when the boy arrived, so he introduced himself. Doris could tell that being around a stranger made Danny uncomfortable, so after the introduction she quickly suggested that they go see the lambs.

When they got to the barn, Arla was already there playing with the young sheep. She was surprised to see the strange boy with Doris, but since Arla was never one to be shy, before long she and Danny were chatting about the lambs and a hundred other things, acting as if they were old friends.

Doris was dying to know how Danny had convinced Winnie to come to the picnic, but she couldn't ask Danny with Arla listening. She bit her tongue and tried to keep up with the conversation they were having. It was obvious that Danny enjoyed the new friend he had found in Arla. Doris didn't think it would be hard to bring Danny into the small town community. He was naturally a friendly, outgoing boy. Only recently had he learned from Winnie not to trust others. But Doris was confident he would change once he realized the townspeople were actually kind. Maybe he would even go to school next term.

Later that afternoon, Doris realized she hadn't asked Danny how he'd managed to talk Winnie into the picnic. But she decided that it didn't really matter after all. The important thing was that they were both coming.

Over the next few days, the Frees were busy preparing for the weekend's picnic. The house buzzed with activity. The girls loved picnics, and the fact that company was coming made it even more special than usual. They could hardly wait.

On Tuesday, Ma and Pa went into town together, dressed in their Sunday clothes. They said they had things to do in preparation for the picnic, but the girls couldn't imagine what they needed in town. After all, the food was planned out already, and even if they had needed anything, it wasn't like they could afford to buy it.

All day the girls wondered about it, each guessing at what special item their folks had gone to town to buy. So they were that much more perplexed when their parents returned empty-handed. Ma and Pa wouldn't say a word, though they both seemed pleased, and Ma flushed with excitement every time someone mentioned the picnic.

As the week progressed, things got even stranger. Various townspeople would stop by the house and go out to the barn and speak with Pa in hushed voices. Or else they would sit at the kitchen table with Ma after she'd pushed the girls out of the house. The girls wondered what was going on, but none of them ever guessed at the plan Ma and Pa were hatching.

On Friday, the girls made the cake and got everything ready so that the next day's preparations would be easy and they could all relax and enjoy themselves. The girls sang songs and danced around the kitchen and yard as they worked. Doris was especially excited, and this made her sisters even more giddy since she was usually the quiet one. The girls had trouble getting to sleep the night before the picnic. Ma and Pa, too, were up late, sitting on the porch talking quietly into the night.

Over the hill, Danny was also awake. He was thinking about the pup that might be with him in his room the next night. He scooted over to the edge of his sleeping mat to make sure there would be room at his feet for Tippy. He also thought about all the delicious food the Frees would have made for the picnic. It had been a long time since Danny had eaten really good home cooking. He thought about how fun it would be to laugh and talk with his new friends. He had spent so little time with others since his parents' death—just Winnie and then Doris more recently. Saturday would be a day to remember for sure.

Winnie's thoughts carried her well into the night for other reasons. Danny had talked her into this picnic so skillfully that she hadn't really thought about it at the time. But now that it was the next day, she questioned why she had agreed to go. It was so long since she'd had a real conversation with anyone besides Doris and Danny. And before Danny's arrival, she had gone for months at a time without hearing a single human voice. It had taken her quite some time to get used to Danny's constant chattering and even to hearing her own voice again.

Winnie didn't know how she'd manage a whole day's worth of conversation with these strangers. But what bothered her most of all was that she didn't have anything to bring to the picnic. She had been such a good cook when she was younger, always bringing well-loved dishes to picnics and sharing her recipes with those who asked. It was embarrassing to be so poor that she couldn't even bring a simple pie.

Winnie had just about convinced herself that she shouldn't go to the picnic after all. But then she started remembering all the fun she'd had at such events as a young woman. She'd laughed easily then and had had many friends. What had happened to them? How had things gone so wrong?

Winnie thought that maybe, just maybe, tomorrow could be the beginning of a better life for her and Danny. Maybe she would have friends again, and then when they had a garden and food of their own, she could invite these new friends to a picnic at her dear house with the bright yellow shutters. After all, the Frees were fine people and seemed like they'd be good folks to have as friends. Winnie decided it was high time she ventured out, held her head high, and reacquainted herself with her neighbors.

Finally she drifted off to sleep, excited and nervous about what the next day would bring.

CHAPTER 18

The Camel's Hump

The next morning, their chores done in record time, the girls were in the yard looking expectantly up the hill when Winnie and Danny walked over it at nine o'clock sharp. The adults would have lots of time to talk and the children to play before it was time to eat lunch.

After Doris finished the introductions, Ma invited Winnie into the kitchen and told the children to stay close to the house because they would be leaving soon. The girls looked at one another in puzzlement—they assumed they'd be having the picnic there.

"Where are we going?" Danny asked Doris, his eyes squinting suspiciously. "Winnie almost didn't even come when she thought the picnic would just be here at your house. Who knows what will happen now! What are you planning, Doris?" Danny couldn't believe Doris had let him down—he had trusted her.

"I don't know where we're going, either. I promise!" Doris insisted. "We thought we'd be staying here for the picnic, too." Then she defended her family. "I'm sure Ma and Winnie are talking things over. They'll work it out. We're going to have a great day no matter where we are, you'll see," she tried to reassure him. "We made a pile of good food, and I'll ask Ma if we can bring Tippy with us." Doris knew Danny would do just about anything to take that pup home, so she skillfully changed the subject. "Do you want to go to the barn to get her now?"

"Sure, I guess," said Danny, not yet convinced of Doris's innocence. He was half aware that Doris was using Tippy to calm him down, but he was too enamored with the idea of having his own dog to much care.

The children were laughing and running around with Tippy when Ma and Winnie came out of the house. Ma had the picnic basket piled high, and Winnie was carrying a bundle of dishes wrapped in a checkered tablecloth. Pa appeared from around the side of the barn, smiling as he pulled the new wagon that he had made out of scrap lumber.

"I've got the wagon ready, so let's load up and we'll get going," Pa called out to Winnie and Ma. Then he turned to the kids. "Victoria, why don't you get that heavy bundle from Miss Winnie and bring it here. Jena, you can bring out the jugs of orangeade. And Danny, I'll bet you could carry that basket over there, couldn't you?"

"Yes sir," Danny replied as he followed Victoria over to the porch steps. Arla inspected the wagon and pronounced it perfect. She was already planning the fun she and Doris would have pulling their dolls around the yard. The wagon was sturdy but gave a bumpy ride on the wheels Pa had sawed out of some planks. He had nailed some old tire rubber to the edges of the wheels to give them some traction in the sandy soil.

Before long, the wagon was loaded up and they set off.

As they walked, Ma, Pa, and Winnie chatted like old friends. The girls, however, had gone quiet, wondering where they were going. But not Danny—he was laughing and running ahead, then falling behind as he played with Tippy. He no longer cared where they were going as long as the pup was coming along.

Arla finally asked the question on everyone's mind. "Where are we going anyway? Is it almost time to eat?"

Pa laughed. "No, Arla, it's not near time to eat. You just finished your breakfast! We're heading to Camel's Hump Bluff. We're going to have our picnic under the big oak tree there, by the cold-water spring. It's a beautiful spot, and there are lots of boulders that we grown-ups can relax on while you kids explore the caves."

Now the girls were absolutely giddy with excitement. They hadn't been to the bluff yet this spring, and it was one of their favorite spots. They often found arrowheads, rocks that had been smoothed into tools, and other items from when Native Americans had lived and hunted in the area decades before. They were surprised to be going so far from the house, though, especially with company. Doris worried that Winnie would get tired after such a long walk. The bluff was a mile from the house, and they would have to walk through the cornfield and part of the cow pasture in order to get there. Winnie hadn't spent much time walking these past few years.

The girls raced ahead with Danny and Tippy and arrived at the oak tree long before the grown-ups. They played and waited for the adults to catch up.

A few minutes later, Ma, Pa, and Winnie arrived, and to Doris's surprise, Winnie didn't seem tired at all. Both she and Danny were surprised at how friendly Winnie was around the Frees. They had expected at least some nervousness and suspicion from her. Winnie even surprised herself with how at ease she felt around her neighbors. It was as if they'd been friends for years.

The adults sat down on the large rocks and relaxed. They enjoyed watching the children dart around looking for treasures. Several times Doris saw her parents give each other sly smiles, as if they shared a special secret. She wondered what it was, but then decided it was probably just that they were happy the day's festivities were going well so far, and she quickly dismissed it.

Arla spent the next few hours pestering her folks every few minutes about whether it was time to eat yet. Danny and Doris played with Tippy and explored a few of the caves along the side of the bluff. They were shallow caves that didn't lead anywhere, but many of them made a nice place to sit. They weren't deep enough to offer much shelter to animals, so there was no danger of finding anything larger than a chipmunk hiding inside, though the girls liked to scare each other with stories of bears and wolves hiding in the dark recesses.

Jena and Victoria set out looking for Native American artifacts. They found some stones that they thought looked like tools, but no arrowheads. Danny was fascinated with the stones and began helping them look for more. On the other side of the bluff, he found a large flat rock and called Jena over to inspect it. The center of the rock was worn down to a shallow bowl. Jena guessed that it was probably used for crushing grain to make flour. They were excited about this find, and together they heaved the rock onto its side and rolled it back to show their parents. Jena was determined to add it to her collection despite Pa's groans of protest over how heavy it would be to cart home. The discussion was cut short because just then Ma announced that it was time to set out the picnic.

Jena laid out the checkered blanket, Ma and Victoria began pulling things out of the large basket, and Pa and Winnie laid out the dishes. Arla and Danny got the tin cups ready for the jug of orangeade. Orangeade and lemonade were the girls' favorite summer treats. The citrus fruits were hard to come by, though, so they were a rare pleasure.

They ate chicken and macaroni salad with homemade mayonnaise and pickled green beans until they were full and lazy. Danny smiled throughout the entire meal; he reckoned he had never been so happy in his whole life. Tippy begged scraps from him and then fell asleep with her head on Danny's lap. Everyone laughed when her large puppy feet twitched as she chased after rabbits or chipmunks or who-knows-what in her puppy dreams. Ma and Winnie talked about recipes, and Winnie agreed to show Ma some helpful canning techniques come fall.

Winnie told Ma about the garden she and Danny had begun to plant, and about how they were working hard on the little house. She explained how kind Doris had been and how she had given Winnie hope for a better life for the first time in many years. Doris blushed but it felt wonderful when Ma smiled at her. Ma was proud of the fine young person Doris had become.

"No, you can't keep a cow like that, Danny," Pa was saying. They were talking about farming, and Danny was taking advantage of the older man's knowledge. "A cow has to have more room to move around—a pasture, not just a stall in a barn. Cows need to get out in the sun and graze."

Danny wanted to learn all he could about crops and animals. He had been raised in a city and knew very little about farm life. He had no one else to discuss these things with and felt quite grown-up speaking to a man this way. It made him miss his own father even more. Pa was impressed with the boy's eagerness and thirst for knowledge. He was indeed determined. Pa wouldn't be surprised at all if this boy was running a real farm by himself in just a few years.

After a time the children went off again to play while the adults napped and talked away the beautiful afternoon. After several games of hide-and-seek and much searching for treasured rocks and tools, the kids needed a rest. They sat in the largest of the caves and lit a small candle. They asked Danny about his life in the city, his parents, and the hard winter that he and Winnie had endured. They chatted about school and friends and bullies and summer vacation.

"I hope Winnie'll let you go to school in the fall," said Doris.

Danny shrugged but didn't answer. He was a bit nervous at the thought of school. He didn't have any nice clothes and hadn't even had a real pair of shoes since arriving in Tomah. He worried about how the other kids would treat a newcomer, especially the nephew of a woman many of the townsfolk thought was strange and mean. He didn't share these worries with the girls, though

Doris could tell he had his doubts. But she wasn't concerned—she knew she'd be able to convince him to attend school, as long as Winnie agreed to it first. And after seeing Winnie with her folks today, Doris decided it wouldn't be that hard of a job after all.

Unable to sit still for very long on this exciting day, the children left the cave and went off to play and explore again. Jena and Victoria decided to search for more treasures while the always-hungry Arla ran to see if there was any food left.

"Come on, girl, don't be afraid," Danny coaxed the pup. Tippy had her paws planted firmly at the opening of the cave and refused to enter. "I will stay right next to you. Come on, you can do it. . . ." He patted his leg invitingly, but Tippy wouldn't budge. The hair on her back was standing on end, and she trembled as Danny lifted her gently and carried her into the cave. Doris stood nearby and watched. The cave fascinated Danny, and he hoped Tippy would get used to it so they could explore it together.

Just then a laughing Jena came running over with Victoria in hot pursuit. "Time for cake!" Jena yelled as she quickly turned and screamed, barely escaping Victoria's outstretched hands.

"Just a few minutes ago when Arla ran off in search of food, I could have sworn I was stuffed and couldn't eat another bite. But now, at the mention of cake, I do believe I have room left after all." Danny patted his stomach and smiled at Doris as he spoke.

"We haven't had cake since the holidays. I sure could

go for some some!" Doris agreed.

The two ran happily to the picnic area, not noticing that little Tippy lingered uncertainly at the opening to the cave.

Arla had filled the jug with cold spring water and hauled it the short distance back to the picnic area with the help of the wagon. Soon the cake was gone, and the picnic basket was emptied of all its goodies.

The group laughed and talked a while longer, happy, relaxed, and full from delicious cake. Winnie promised the children that she would make pickled eggs for the next picnic. She also agreed to teach the girls how to make lacy necklaces by tying small knots in strands of thread. They were excited to learn this and begged for the picnic to be held the following weekend. The adults laughed and told them that there was too much work to do on their farms to picnic the following weekend, but that the next one would be soon.

Suddenly Danny jumped to his feet. He looked around anxiously. "Tippy? Tippy?" he called. He panicked when the pup didn't appear and began running around the picnic area, searching for the dog behind the boulders at the bottom of the bluff.

Danny returned to the blanket. "Does anyone see her?" he asked tearfully.

Then the girls became worried too, and jumped up to join the search, all of them talking at once and looking around wildly.

"Everyone, calm down!" Pa's voice boomed over their heads. The girls stopped and looked at him expectantly. "Danny, where did you last see Tippy?" he continued.

"By the cave. Before we came to eat cake," Danny croaked. His face had turned white, and he was breathless with worry and fear.

"Okay, Danny, you and Doris go back to the cave and look around there. Jena and Victoria, you search the edge of the woods. Arla and I will look over the other side of the bluff, and Ma and Winnie, you wait here in case Tippy comes back. Whoever finds her, bring her back to the blanket and wait for the others to return." Pa made a sweeping gesture with his arm, sending them all off to their assigned search locations.

Despite Pa's instruction to stay calm, the children were all jumpy as they ran off. Danny was devastated. He'd waited so long to have a puppy of his own, and now his dream was crushed before his dog had even had the chance to see her new home or to sleep at her master's feet.

On the other side of the bluff, Pa and Arla had just entered a thicket of trees when a haunting howl filled the afternoon air. Pa recognized the sound at once, but Arla was too busy looking and yelling for the puppy to hear it. It was a coyote. Usually they only howled at night, and Pa hadn't heard one this close to his farm in a long time. It sounded as if the coyote was at the top of the bluff.

Despite Arla's protest he turned her around and suggested that they head back. "The puppy didn't come this way," he insisted, hoping Arla wouldn't argue. She trusted her father's judgment and didn't question why their search was so brief.

As they approached the picnic area, Pa hoped to see Tippy scampering around with a laughing Danny chasing her. Instead they ran into the rest of the children heading back to the blanket empty-handed. They were approaching Ma and Winnie wearing sad expressions when Pa heard another coyote howl.

Pa looked at Danny. The boy was trying hard not to cry. "We'll find her, Danny, don't you worry," Pa reassured him. But he didn't really believe it. He doubted they'd ever see the tumbling pup again. With a hungry coyote around, Tippy didn't stand a chance.

Pa would come back later with his gun and shoot the coyote before it started killing his and his neighbors' chickens, but there was nothing to do about it now. This day, which had started out as a wonderful and relaxing time, was now tainted with sadness and loss. Pa knew it would be even harder on the children if he insisted that they go home immediately, so instead he suggested that they look for Tippy a little longer.

To keep everyone safe and to ensure that no one stumbled upon any gruesome remains, Pa ordered everyone to stay together, and then he walked ahead of the group. They made a slow sweep of the area, staying in the open and taking turns calling to the puppy. Tippy failed show herself, despite the pleading calls.

After an hour more of searching, Pa announced, to everyone's dismay, that the sun was starting to go down and it was time to head back so Winnie and Danny could get home before dark. "Don't you kids worry. We'll come back first thing tomorrow and look some more. Maybe Tippy is just trapped somewhere and can't get out. We'll find her."

The children were grief-stricken. They hated the idea of leaving the puppy alone in the woods for the night. Ma and Winnie, on the other hand, had recognized the howl as that of a coyote and they, like Pa, doubted the puppy would be found. But Ma didn't want to let on to the kids. "Maybe Tippy had a bellyache from all the food you children were sneaking to her. Let's go home and see if she ran ahead and is waiting for us there."

Although no one thought it likely that Tippy would have left the picnic and returned to the farm alone, they welcomed any glimmer of hope. Everyone began gathering their things for the long walk home.

As Doris was packing the plates in the picnic basket, she looked over at Ma and Pa, who were folding the blanket together. They were whispering, and she could've sworn she saw them smile at one another. Could she have imagined it? How could they smile about anything right now? She knew they both must be worried about Tippy, yet they had that look—they were hiding something.

CHAPTER 19

Miracle

The children lagged behind on the walk home in an attempt to both prolong their time together and give Tippy a chance to catch up. Jena had talked Pa into hauling the huge Native American grinding stone back to the house, and the wagon shook under its weight as he tugged it over the bumpy cornfield.

The children looked behind them often as they walked. Everyone was silent, and the trip back home from Camel's Hump Bluff seemed much longer than the walk there had.

When the house was finally in sight, Doris noticed an unfamiliar wagon pulled up next to it. She looked at her pa. He glanced at the wagon but didn't seem concerned about it, which was odd. Then Doris spotted something even stranger: two more wagons were heading away from the house, and Ma and Pa were pretending not to notice. Instead, they turned and talked to Winnie, who was looking down to keep from tripping. Winnie never even noticed the wagons.

Jena glanced at Victoria and silently mouthed the words, "Who's that?" Victoria answered with a shrug.

Because Danny was continually looking back for Tippy, he hadn't noticed the wagons or the perplexed looks being shot back and forth between the Free girls. No one asked the questions that were on their minds, because they didn't want to alarm their new friends. It was obvious that Ma and Pa were keeping quiet on purpose, so the girls figured there was a good reason why.

When it looked like Arla was about to say something, Doris put her finger to her lips and mouthed "Shh." Arla looked down and pursed her lips together tightly, as if it was actually painful for her to keep the words in.

"Well, I think I've pulled this rock far enough for now," Pa grunted when they'd almost reached the farm. "I'll leave the wagon here and tow it the rest of the way in the morning. Girls, let's escort our neighbors home, okay?" He turned to look at the girls and gave them a wink as if they shared a secret, but in truth the girls had no idea what was happening. Their curiosity over their father's odd behavior even caused them to forget about the puppy for a moment. Danny, however, continued looking hopefully toward the Frees' farm for any sign of Tippy.

"Okay, Pa," Arla perked up. "Can we run ahead?" Arla lived in the moment and rarely noticed when something strange was going on.

"No," Pa said a bit too quickly, "let's all walk together and while we do, you girls can talk about when the next picnic should be with Winnie and Danny."

Danny blinked his eyes as if he just now realized where he was. He'd been too preoccupied with Tippy's whereabouts to pay attention to what was going on. But now he spoke up, and there was pride in his voice that mingled with sadness. "The picnic will have to wait until I get our garden hoed and planted. We have a lot to do if we are going to have vegetables to put up for next winter."

"I understand that, Danny," Pa said, putting a hand on the boy's shoulder as they began walking up the hill.

The girls, however, were too sad and tired to plan anything just now, so they walked in silence.

For his part, Danny was crushed about how the day had turned out. He loved Camel's Hump Bluff and he was happy about his new friendship with the Free family, but he could think of nothing but Tippy. *Things were going so well. Why did Tippy have to run off and ruin everything?* he wondered. Anger began to seep in.

They reached the top of the hill, and Winnie glanced down to take in the little house with its graying wood and bright yellow shutters that she loved. Winnie gasped and halted, staring wide-eyed at the scene before her.

Jena, Victoria, and Arla hadn't seen the house for years—since a friend had dared them to get close enough to Witch Winnie's house to steal ivy from its side—so they weren't aware of the change. But when they heard Winnie's gasp and felt Doris and Danny stiffen, they understood that the house was not as it had been that morning.

Danny stood in confused silence, unable to register what he saw. It wasn't long, however, before words returned to him. "This is a miracle!" he hooted, jumping around wildly. It was the first time he'd smiled in hours. Then, as he was bouncing around, he heard a familiar yelp coming from behind him. He spun around so fast that he lost his balance and tumbled over.

Everyone else turned to the sound. Trotting up behind them, panting from the effort of trying to catch up, was a filthy, soaking Tippy. She was covered in a thick mud that could only have come from one of the caves. But they didn't care where she had been, just that she was back. Their eyes shone with happy tears.

Danny couldn't believe what was happening. Two dreams of his—to own a puppy and to live on a real farm—seemed to be coming true before his eyes. He looked back and forth between Tippy and the house, unsure about which to run to first. He decided on the muddy puppy—after all, the farm wasn't going anywhere, but you never knew about Tippy. He hugged the dog and was rewarded with licks and a happy bark.

Doris thought Tippy seemed pleased with all of the attention she was getting. "You naughty pup! You've been nothing but trouble. It's a good thing you have a master now to teach you some manners," she teased. Everyone laughed, and the sound was musical after the heavy silence during the walk home. Then the group's attention refocused on the house and farm at the bottom of the hill. They were transformed almost beyond belief.

"This sure is a miracle," Pa chuckled. "A miracle set into motion by the kindness of Doris Free, who cared and helped when no one else even stopped to talk to this family. She is a generous, wonderful person."

Doris stared wide-eyed at her father. "But, Pa, I didn't do this. It doesn't even seem possible. We were only gone for the day...." She trailed off, bewildered by what had happened.

Winnie was still staring, frozen to the spot. Tears rolled

off her cheek and spotted her dress. Finally she started down the hill, and the rest of them followed. Doris glanced at Winnie, wondering what emotions were behind those tears. Were they happy tears? Or were they tears of outrage over other people meddling in her life?

Because what they saw barely resembled the residence Winnie and Danny had left that morning. The house had been painted snow white, and the yellow shutters shone like the sun against it. There were flowers in new window boxes on the side of the house. Several snowball bushes and other flowering plants lined the house beautifully. But the house was just the beginning.

Next to the house was a garden—not a small kitchen garden, but a large garden tilled and planted in neat rows. Each row was still moist with the water that had been sprinkled onto the newly planted seeds. Little sticks marked each row and announced what type of plant would soon sprout. Doris saw potatoes, onions, corn, four kinds of beans, peas, tomatoes, pumpkins, and squash.

The barn that had been hopelessly run-down was now fully repaired and gleamed with a new coat of red paint. Danny and Tippy now ran toward it with abandon. Large brown letters in a white frame proudly spelled out *Stephens* on the side of the barn. A small corral had been built on to the back, and there was a young horse inside nibbling a bale of hay. Next to the corral was a small pen with two sheep in it bleating softly; Danny stopped just long enough to rub each sheep's head.

He was running around the place like a dust devil, trying to take it all in—both to understand it and to make certain it was real. Tippy followed him everywhere, investigating her new home. It was exactly like he had imagined their farm would be...and it had all just suddenly appeared on one magical day.

"Cows!" Danny proclaimed loudly from the barn. "Two new milk cows and a bull calf. And the cutest little piglets you ever saw, Winnie—three of 'em!"

Doris giggled at Tippy who was barking at the wagging cow tails in the barn. It was all just too much. Ma and Pa smiled and began to laugh. Soon they were all chuckling at the wonder of it all. Everyone except for Winnie, that is. Doris still wasn't sure if the woman was happy about all of this. It was an intrusion, after all, and if there was anyone who didn't like being intruded upon, it was Winnie.

But Doris's thoughts soon returned to the farm itself. How had all of this been accomplished in a single day? How could her parents have been involved when they were at the picnic all day?

Just then, Danny came running out of the house so giddy with excitement that he was shaking. He plowed into Winnie, but she was like a statue. She didn't speak or even look at him; she just continued to stare at her house. Danny had his arms around her, and a flood of words was pouring from his mouth. "There is food in the kitchen, Winnie, piles of it. There are canned vegetables and canned meats and even some fruit. There's flour and sugar and spices and yeast. On the table is a stack of towels and blankets, and there are some extra chairs so we can even have company. There's a basket full of yarn, and the wood box is plumb full!"

Then Danny began to cry—not quiet tears of joy, but

a powerful bawling that shook his whole body. Finally the emotions he'd held inside for so long were surfacing. He cried over his dead parents, over moving to a strange place, over being poor and hungry for so long, and over months and months of being friendless and hopeless.

He cried because Doris had brought him hope, along with her compassion and gifts. And he cried because his dream of having a real farm—and a puppy of his own— had finally come true. It was all too much to bear.

Then Winnie looked at Pa and met his eyes. There was bewilderment and hurt there, but not anger. She didn't speak, but her expression made it clear that it was time for Pa to explain what had happened on this amazing day.

"Let's go inside so we can sit down and talk about all of this," Pa said quietly and comfortingly. He put his hand on Winnie's arm, guided her to the house, and led the way into her home.

CHAPTER 20

Season of Promise

There were so many new things in the house it was as if they'd mistakenly entered the wrong place.

"Well, I guess I'll start at the beginning and then you can ask questions, okay?" Pa softly said to Winnie after she had lit a lantern and placed it on the table.

There was a pad of paper on the table and written on it were orders for blankets. The yarn Danny had mentioned was for Winnie to weave blankets to sell to the townspeople. The money would help keep up the farm. Winnie once again had a place in the town. She would be able to make her own way and hold on to her pride.

Pa began. "A few weeks ago, Doris came to us and told us about you and Danny—how you were living out here without much of anything. We didn't even know that Danny was here, so of course we were all surprised about that."

He cleared his throat and continued. "We are aware of what happened when your husband died, and I for one was ashamed that the whole town stood by and let it occur. Doris told us how she had tried to help you, and she defended you. The townspeople of Tomah had turned you into an outcast and a prisoner in your own home, and it took an innocent child to realize your goodness." Pa paused and looked from Winnie to Doris.

Winnie took a deep breath and spoke in a voice wobbly with tears. "Your little Doris is the first person to visit without taking anything from me in a long time. She spoke kindly and sat and laughed with me and Danny while I made rugs to sell for garden seed. She told Danny how to find useful things at the dump. I had lost all hope, and my dreams for Danny's future were fading away, but then Doris brought us some warm eggs and everything changed. When the chicks hatched, so too did new hope in our hearts. We started planning and building, and I knew that together, Danny and I could do anything."

Winnie paused for a moment, gathered herself, and continued. "We became a family after Doris entered our lives, Mr. Free. That's what we did—we became a family. Now how is it that this one little girl caused all of this magic to occur? Surely she had some help. Because as far as I can recall, this little lady was with us the whole day and not here painting a barn and making cows appear out of thin air!"

Everyone laughed, relieved that Winnie wasn't angry. Pa continued with a sigh. "The day after Doris told us about you, we went to town and spoke with the town council. I felt terrible about what had happened to you, and I thought it was time to make amends. We called a meeting that night and didn't tell anyone what it was about until they'd arrived. One hundred and fifty people showed up, and preacher Williams gave a brief speech about helping your neighbor, which he ended with one name: Winnie Stephens. With your name hanging in the air, everyone started squirming in their seats. They all knew they had done wrong by you."

Winnie looked down as though ashamed, but Dad continued with his explanation.

"You didn't do anything wrong to any of them, ever. Yet they all took revenge on you for what your husband did. You were a widow with no family around to help or defend you. The entire town acted horribly—including people like me, who took nothing, but who also didn't try to stop others from doing so. Then preacher Williams started naming names. 'Mr. Thompson,' he said, 'how many sheep have you raised from the sheep you took from that innocent woman? And Mr. Clay, how long did those cows give you milk and calves?' On and on he went about everything you lost to the vengeful people of this town."

Winnie's eyes were full of mixed emotions. "I know my husband owed these people. It was wrong what he did. I don't blame the townsfolk for being angry...but what they did to me...they left me with nothing. It has been so hard." Silent tears of hard memories and loneliness snaked down her cheeks, but there was still a note of pride in her uplifted chin—after all, she had survived.

"You have a wonderful spirit, Winnie, and a forgiving heart. That's what has carried you through. After preacher Williams shamed dozens of people over what they had done, he called out to those who had done nothing at all, not only by turning their heads while this was happening, but also in the years that followed while you were alone and hungry. Not a single person offered relief to you, or even friendship. He had everyone crying, and that's when we started planning.

"It quickly blossomed into the biggest workday ever planned. I don't even know how many people were here today, probably at least a hundred from the looks of things. They tilled your fields and planted them. Your plow has been returned to you in good repair, and your toolshed is full. You will have feed for those animals this winter, and the townspeople will make sure your fields are harvested until Danny is old enough to take over the work.

"The animals, though, are his responsibility. I will teach him how to care for them properly and deliver the young that are sure to come over the next few years. These are hard times, and many people are going without during this depression, but when we all joined together, we were able to come up with everything that you would need to make a go of it and to return all that was taken from you."

Pa continued, "I'm sorry for all that happened to you, Winnie, and I know that this doesn't erase it, but I hope that you will find it in your heart to forgive the people of Tomah. We would like to have a ceremony tomorrow to welcome Danny to our community and to welcome you back. We have cheated ourselves out of your company for long enough. I hope you'll come. This is a season of promise, Winnie."

Epilogue

The season of promise was as joyous as each of them dreamed it would be. Winnie and Danny quickly became respected members of the community, and that summer, Winnie's recipes were once again the talk of all of the picnics and fairs.

It was in the fall that Winnie began to plant daffodils as her symbol of thankfulness to the people of Tomah—especially for Doris and the seed of hope that she had planted in Winnie's heart. Winnie planted the flowers on hillsides and roadsides and along fields. She planted more bulbs every fall. When people asked her when she would be finished planting, she would get a faraway look in her eyes and tell them the story of a little girl who didn't give up on a grouchy old woman and a dirty little boy. Then she would dig into her basket for another bulb and continue planting.

About the Great Depression

The Great Depression began on October 29, 1929. On this day, which became known as Black Tuesday, the value of the stock market dropped rapidly, or "crashed." Thousands of people who had invested in the stock market lost money—many lost their entire savings. Banks closed across the country. Stores and factories closed too, leaving people jobless and penniless. Many people didn't have enough money to pay their bills or even to buy food.

People living in farming communities, like the Free family, often got by better than people in larger cities, because they were used to fending for themselves. Farming families grew their own food and raised animals for milk, meat, and to help with farm work. They learned to use each item until it could be used no more, and they were especially careful not to waste food.

The Depression affected everyone in the United States, and its effects were felt throughout the world. Herbert Hoover was president when the Depression started. It lasted from October 1929 until the 1940s. The start of World War II finally caused the Depression to end. The war created many jobs—soldiers needed weapons, clothing, ships, and airplanes. These jobs gave people the money they needed to pay their bills and get back on their feet. They started buying things again, stores reopened, and the economy slowly rebounded.